Catching HIM

Shooting Stars Series

Fighting to Breathe
Wide Open Spaces
One Last Wish

Fluke My Life Series

Running into Love
Stumbling into Love
Tossed into Love
Drawn into Love

Ruby Falls Series

Falling Fast

Writing as C. A. Rose

Alfha Law Series

Justified
Liability
Verdict

Stand-Alone Title

Finders Keepers

Catching HIM

Aurora Rose Reynolds

Published by Montlake Romance, Seattle
www.apub.com

Amazon, the Amazon logo, and Montlake Romance are trademarks of Amazon.com, Inc., or its affiliates.

ISBN-13: 9781542005371
ISBN-10: 154200537X

Cover design by Letitia Hasser

Cover photography by Wander Aguiar Photography

Printed in the United States of America

*Kayla, thank you for your unwavering friendship,
support, and encouragement.*

Suggestion 1

ADOPT THE UNADOPTABLE CAT

LEAH

I pick up my cat from his perch on the window ledge before I open the front door to check my mailbox. Since I'm not dressed yet, I stay inside and reach one hand out while I hold Mouse's small wiggling body firmly against me with the other. I flip the lid and start to reach into the box but stop and wrap my arms around him when he squirms to get down.

"No way, sir. Not today." My hold on him tightens, but it's not enough. He slips from my grasp, and I watch in slow motion as he lands on all four paws, takes off across my porch, and then heads down the three steps into the yard. "Mouse!"

He stops to look at me over his furry gray shoulder, like he's asking, *What?*

"Come on, baby. Come here." I start toward him slowly, hoping that if I'm slow I can get close enough to grab him. He tips his head to the side, blinking at me, before he takes off again toward the house next door. "Mouse, get your furry butt back here!" I yell, rushing across the cool grass in my bare feet and wearing nothing but a tank top and plain panties. I glimpse his tail as he runs to the back of the house next door, and I pick up speed, only to stop suddenly once I turn the corner and spot him sitting on the ledge of an open window, licking his paw.

"Please don't do this," I beg him, taking careful steps in his direction. "Please, just stop." I hold up my hands like I'm dealing with a terrorist set on detonating a bomb instead of my stubborn cat. I take another slow, calculated step and then cry "No!" when he turns and hops through the window, disappearing inside.

"This cannot be happening." I run a hand through my knotted bed head hair and look around for something to use to get my ass up and through the window. If my old neighbors, Margret and Ethan, still lived here, I would've just knocked on their door and had them get Mouse for me, but they moved six months ago. Since then, the house has been empty.

A large bright-orange bucket near the back deck catches my eye, so I dump out the dirty water that's settled in the bottom, then carry it to the window. After setting it upside down, I place one foot on it, testing its stability, before doing the same with my other foot and lifting the window up completely. When I poke my head in, I look around the dimly lit empty room and narrow my eyes on Mouse, who's sitting casually by an open door like he's been waiting for me.

"Get a cat. They aren't much work, and you need company." Why the hell did I listen to my mother . . . again? I grumble to myself as I pull myself through the window, grouching and wincing as the old dry wood and paint scrape my belly, my thighs, and my shins. I cry out, more from shock than from pain, as I land on the floor with a loud thud.

"Just so you know, I'm totally rethinking our relationship," I say, turning my head toward Mouse. I freeze when my eyes catch the glint of a gun aimed in my direction.

"What the fuck?" is growled as the overhead light is flipped on, and I scream like a chick in a horror movie who's being chased through the woods by an ax murderer. "Jesus, I'm not gonna fucking shoot you," a deep voice says, and I peek out from between my fingers, which are covering my face. I freeze again for a completely different reason once I see the guy standing over me.

Holy moly.

I blink, trying to clear my vision to make sure I'm not imagining him. Tan skin, dark, almost-black hair that curls around his ears and neck, a strong jaw, full lips. Add to that broad shoulders and six-pack abs that are visible because he's totally shirtless and totally right in front of me, wearing nothing but a pair of gray sweats.

"What the fuck are you doing breaking into my house?" he barks, and I pull my eyes away from his and look around for the reason I broke into his house. "Hello . . . ?" he calls when I don't respond, sounding annoyed.

"Umm." I frown when I don't spot the reason for me being in this stupid mess.

Feeling heat hit my legs and chest, I look up, and my eyes flare when I notice his gaze on me . . . all of me. I quickly pull down my tank top as far as it'll go, then hold my hand to my chest to cover my exposed cleavage.

"I live next door, and my cat—"

He cuts me off, frowning. "What?"

"My cat came in through the window. I . . ." I look around again. "I followed him in."

"You could've knocked on the door."

"I—"

"Are you crazy?"

"I—"

"Must be crazy." He shakes his head, and I narrow my eyes.

Okay, yeah, I messed up by breaking into his house, but he's seriously starting to piss me off by cutting me off and calling me crazy. Plus, I didn't even know this was his house—or anyone's, for that matter.

"I'm not crazy." I put my hands behind me and heft my booty up off the ground. "I didn't know you lived here. I didn't know anyone moved in. The house has been empty for months."

"So you're telling me you missed the big-ass yellow moving truck parked in the driveway?" he questions, and I bite my lip, because I obviously did miss the big-ass yellow moving truck parked in the driveway. "You also missed that the For Sale sign was taken from the front lawn weeks ago?"

Okay, I missed that too. Then again, I haven't really been paying attention.

"Oops." I roll my lips together, and his eyes drop to my mouth before he pulls them away to look up at the ceiling, muttering something under his breath I can't make out.

I look down at my feet when something soft glides along my ankles, and I see Mouse. I quickly scoop him up and hold him tightly against my chest. "Bad kitty," I say, and he rubs his face against my jaw, purring. "You're definitely living up to your reputation."

I'm unable to stop myself from kissing the top of his furry head. In his defense, the pound did warn me about him. They said he was shifty and free spirited and that I would have to keep an eye on him because he's a runner, which is why every time he's been adopted, he's been brought back to the pound. "You're lucky you're so cute." I kiss his head again.

"Do you always talk to your cat?"

Crap, how did I forget where I was or who I was with? "Not always." I don't look up at him because I don't want him to see how pink my cheeks are.

"I think I read somewhere that crazy people talk to their animals," he says, and my eyes fly up to his.

"Jerk."

"Just saying." He smirks.

I snap, "Can I use your front door?"

His smirk turns into a lazy grin, and his eyes scour the length of me, making my skin feel hot. "I don't know." He shrugs one bare shoulder. "I'm kinda tempted to watch you crawl back out the way you came in."

"You . . . you . . . I don't even know what you are!" I sputter as my cheeks get warm.

He laughs, throwing his head back in hilarity. "Lucky for you, sweetheart, I feel like being a gentleman." He turns for the door, still laughing, and I glare daggers at his back as I follow him out of the room and down a long hall to the front door. He turns to face me, and I hold my head high and continue glaring at him as I march past him out the door. "See you around."

"Don't count on it!" I shout over my shoulder, lifting my hand to flip him the bird, but I stop when Mouse starts to wiggle away from me again. I fumble with my cat in the jerk's front yard, trying to get ahold of him while listening to the loud, obnoxious laughter behind me. When I finally have Mouse firmly in my grasp, I quicken my steps and head up my porch and then right through my front door. I drop Mouse back on his perch before going to the couch and falling back onto it.

I close my eyes, then open them back up when Mouse jumps up to my chest. "Let's make a deal." I lift him up to get his full attention. "From now on, you only run out of the house when I'm dressed and have brushed my hair."

"Meowww." He reaches out and paws my nose.

"It was worth a shot." I sit up and tuck him under my chin. "On the plus side, I doubt Mr. Hottie next door is going to forget me any-time soon." I sigh and then continue on a mumble, "On the not-so-plus side, I doubt Mr. Hottie next door is going to forget me anytime soon."

"Meowww," Mouse agrees, and I don't know if that's good or bad.

Suggestion 2

Avoid, Avoid, Avoid, Or At Least Try To

LEAH

When I pull into my driveway, I automatically look at the house next door, glancing away quickly when I notice my new neighbor getting out of a large black truck. I know I should acknowledge him—give him a friendly wave or even stop to ask if he's settling in okay—but I don't. Instead, I quickly hit the remote for my garage door and glide my car inside, letting out a relieved breath when the door closes behind me.

My father would be disappointed. He's always saying, "Leah, honey, you need to be friendly with the people you live around. They're the ones who are closest to you if something bad ever happens." Normally, I would agree with him, and with all my other neighbors, I've adhered to his advice. I've always made a point to be welcoming when someone new moves to my block; I take over cookies, introduce myself, and suggest we exchange numbers just in case there's ever an emergency. I can admit I've been less than welcoming to the guy next door ever since I broke into his house to rescue my cat.

For a week, I've been doing everything within my power to avoid another run-in. I check to see if he's outside before I even open my door to get my mail, and I never go out when I see him working in his yard, which he seems to do a lot. Okay, so I might spy on him from behind my curtains, but there's not a woman alive who wouldn't watch him working in his yard wearing a backward baseball cap, his shirt plastered to his big body.

Mouse runs my way and circles my feet when I get into my house. On my way to my bedroom, I pause briefly and scoop him up in my arms, kissing his head even as he hisses and bats his tiny paws at me. He's been angry at me, mad that he's cooped up within the confines of the house when there's so much for him to explore outside. I see him eyeing me and the door every day, like he's waiting for me to slip up so he can make his escape. I've been extra cautious over the past week, because the first chance he gets he's going to disappear, and with my luck, he's going to disappear right into my neighbor's house, through the window that seems to always be left open.

In my bedroom, I strip out of the all-black clothing I wear to the salon that I co-own with my mom and grandmother. A salon that's been a part of our town for over twenty years. Growing up, I planned on becoming a nurse and ended up getting my practical-nursing license and working in a hospital. But after three years of passing out pills, writing in charts, and witnessing death so regularly that it became normal, I decided nursing just wasn't for me. I wasn't really happy, so I quit my job and started working at the salon while I tried to figure out my calling.

I honestly didn't expect that working alongside my mother and grandmother would be my passion, but it is, and long story short, I went to cosmetology school and became a stylist. After I graduated, I officially joined the family business and have worked at Bleach Bomb Shell's—named after my grandmother, Shelly—for the last five years.

I love my job, even though there are days when working with my mother pushes me to the edge of insanity. My mom acts like a typical mother: in my business, slightly nagging, and concerned I'll spend the rest of my life alone with no man to take care of me, because, in her words, I "don't date enough."

At thirty-three, I've had a few boyfriends but just two semiserious relationships. One in high school, and the most recent, Chris, lasted two years before I threw in the towel and ended it about a year ago. Chris was great when he wasn't sending me mixed messages by telling me one month that he wanted to be with me and he'd never been happier and the next month not knowing if he wanted something so serious or was ready to commit. I couldn't understand why a thirty-nine-year-old man had issues committing, especially when it seems normal to be married with children by thirty-five. After the last time he gave me the same run-around about commitment and our long-term prospects, I told him he could have all the time he needed to figure things out, because I was done.

That relationship taught me that chasing a man isn't the way to catch one. My grandmother always says that if a man is interested in you, he'll make that clear without any kind of games, and after Chris, I finally listened. Where that man is I don't know, but I'm hoping he shows up before I'm fifty and I've adopted five more cats.

Shaking off those thoughts, I change into a pair of jeans and a sweatshirt, then head to the kitchen for something to eat. Just like yesterday when I looked in my pantry and fridge, I have no food. Well, I do have food. I have a ton of cat food, a box of crackers, and a bit of hummus. I hate grocery shopping. Shopping for clothes or house goods I love. Grocery shopping I avoid like the plague. I have no real self-control, and I always end up with a cartful of junk food, then feel guilty when I eat nothing but garbage for a week straight. Maybe it would help if I didn't go when I'm starving and think that every item in a colorful box looks delicious.

Knowing I can't avoid the unavoidable unless I want to eat crackers and hummus for dinner, I pick up my purse and car keys, then head back to the garage.

At the grocery store, I grab a cart and head inside, telling myself that I'll stick to the outer section of the store. I heard on one of the early-morning shows that you should avoid the inner aisles, that everything you really need is on the perimeter—fruits, veggies, meats, and dairy.

As I'm halfway through the store and feeling good about my choices, a bright-red box catches my attention. I know I shouldn't gravitate to it, but I can't help it. Fruity Pebbles are my weakness; there is nothing more delicious than a big bowl of the colorful cereal and ice-cold milk. After I grab the largest box I can find, I'm completely thrown off course. The inner aisles suck me in, and once more I end up checking out with a cartful of junk food. Thankfully, I did get some fruit, so I don't feel so guilty.

I pack up my car and head home, driving down the main drag past all the local businesses, including the salon. Mount Pleasant is a typical South Carolina town. It's filled with tourists, but the locals all know each other since most have been here for years. Having traveled often, I can say with authority that there is nowhere more welcoming.

When I drive onto my block, I wave at a few of my neighbors who are outside enjoying the fall weather. I pull into my driveway and frown at a large black dog lying on my front porch. Wondering who the dog belongs to, I pull into the garage. I swing my car door open as the garage door goes down, then let out a scream when the dog appears at my side, startling me.

"Nice puppy," I say in what I hope is a soothing tone when the dog starts toward me. Its tail begins to wag, and I let out the breath I was holding while I reach out my hand. "Good puppy." I scratch the top of its dark head, which hits almost the middle of my stomach. "Who do you belong to?" I ask, checking its collar for a tag. When I find one, I read the front and smile at him. "Hey, Bruce."

He barks, making me jump, and then nudges my hand to give him another rubdown. I pet the top of his head, then flip the tag over and read the name and number on the other side. I pull out my phone and call Tyler Duncan, leave a message with my name and number, and tell him I have his dog.

"I don't know how my cat's going to feel about you coming into the house," I tell Bruce, rubbing his head. "Do you like cats?" He sits with a groan and tips his head to the side like he's thinking about my question. "I mean for more than just snacking on."

He lets out a huff, like he's saying, *As if,* and I smile.

"You're going to have to wait here for a few minutes while I get my groceries inside and lock Mouse in my room."

With another groan, he lies down near my trunk. I unpack my car, carrying everything inside in one trip, because I also hate lugging in groceries. After I'm done, I go in search of Mouse, who's asleep in his bed, which is suction cupped to the window in the dining room. I carry him to my bedroom and deposit him on the bed before shutting the door.

I bring Bruce inside, and he sniffs around for a few minutes before ending up in front of my bedroom door. Mouse, on the opposite side, reaches his tiny kitty paws under in an attempt to get out, and Bruce thinks it's a game and begins to try to catch them. Not seeing any aggression between the two, I leave them and go to the kitchen to put away the groceries. As I start to make myself some dinner, I call the number for Bruce's owner again and leave another message. Bruce smells the sautéing chicken and comes into the kitchen. He looks up at the stove, then at me.

"I don't have any dog food, buddy," I tell him, and I swear he pouts. "If I have to go out and get you some food, I will, but I'm hoping your owner will realize you're missing and call me back before that."

I watch him turn around in a circle and flop down on my kitchen floor, and then I go back to the stove and flip over the chicken as my cell phone on the counter rings. It's a local number, so I slide my finger across the screen, then put my phone to my ear. "Hello?"

"You left a message that you have my dog," says a deep, attractive, and somewhat familiar voice. I look down at Bruce, who has his head on his paws and his eyes on me.

"Yes, he was on my front porch when I got home. He came into my garage after I pulled my car in, which I didn't realize until after I shut the garage door. He scared me to death, but he's sweet, and I didn't want to put him back outside since he obviously belongs to someone," I ramble.

"Shit. Sorry about that. He's never taken off before," he says, and I hear what sounds like a door slamming. "I just got in my truck. I'll come get him. Where are you located?"

Why is his voice so familiar? Why do I think I know him? I shake my head and rattle off my address.

"You've got to be shitting me." He laughs.

"Pardon?"

"Never mind. I'll be right there." He hangs up, and my heart starts to race.

I look at Bruce. "No way." When the doorbell rings not even a minute later, I tip my head back to face the ceiling and groan, hoping I'm wrong. When I drop my head forward, I watch Bruce get up. "You just had to belong to the guy next door, didn't you?"

He barks in response, wiggling with excitement as he walks toward me. I rub his head and then pat my leg. "Come on. Your dad's here to get you."

He follows me to the door, then sits at my side as I swing it open.

Mr. Hottie from next door, now known as Tyler, smirks down at me from under the bill of his baseball cap. "Babe, you didn't need to kidnap my dog just to get my attention," he jokes.

I cross my arms over my chest while glaring at him and huff. "As if I want your attention."

He laughs and looks down at Bruce, who hasn't made a move toward him. His brows pull together, and he pats his leg. "Come on, bud." Bruce moves only enough to turn his big head and lick my hand. "How long has he been over here?"

"Maybe an hour?" I shrug, placing my hand on Bruce's furry head when he rests his heavy weight against my side. I scratch behind his ears. "Are you sure he's yours? Maybe you're trying to kidnap him before his real owner returns." I smirk, and his eyes narrow on my mouth.

"He's mine."

"Doesn't seem like it." I shrug again, getting a kick out of annoying him as much as he annoyed me the last time we were in each other's presence. Obviously Bruce is his; his name and number are on the tag.

He opens his mouth to reply, but Bruce barks, grabbing our attention, and gets up. I follow him through the living room and down the hall, and my eyes widen when he goes right to my bedroom door and lifts his front half off the ground. His big paw knocks down the L-shaped handle, and when his paws slide down the door, it swings inward. Mouse takes his opportunity to escape and flies from the room, zooming past Bruce and then me.

I dive for my cat and shout, "Shut the front door!" but miss him by a mile. I groan as I land on my knees, watching him escape with Bruce chasing after him right out the still-open front door and past a stunned Tyler. Before I'm prepared, I'm lifted right off the floor and tightly tucked into a warm chest that smells way too good. "Please tell me your dog isn't going to eat my cat," I say while tipping my head back to look into Tyler's too-gorgeous eyes.

"I hope not," he says in return, looking somewhat worried. I push away from him, swearing I feel his arms tighten before he finally lets me go. I step around his huge body and run out of the house and down the steps of my porch, with Tyler behind me.

I can hear a dog barking, so I run toward the sound. I make a left around the corner of my house and come to a sliding stop when I see Bruce. His paws are up on the ledge of an open window of Tyler's house, and he's barking at Mouse, who's just out of reach and looking down at him.

"Shit, I forgot to shut the window after I finished painting that room," Tyler says from my side.

I look up at him. "Really? It's been open for a week. Someone could've broken in and stolen everything from you."

"If you saw it's been open, gorgeous, you should have said something," he responds, making me feel guilty.

I look away, mumbling, "How was I supposed to know you didn't leave it open on purpose?"

"Fuck, you're cute." He chuckles, grabbing my hand and dragging me with him toward the window. I try to pull away after a tingling sensation shoots through our connected hands and my belly, but he doesn't let go. Instead, his hand tightens.

"Bruce, heel," he orders, and Bruce immediately lowers his front paws to the ground and looks between us with his tail wagging. "Good boy." He takes us closer to Bruce and the window.

My eyes are zeroed in on Mouse, who's watching us, and I read his next move before he even makes it. "Don't do it," I hiss. His golden eyes blink at me before he leaps into Tyler's house.

"Well, at least he's in there and not out on the street somewhere," Tyler says.

"Yeah." I try to tug my hand free but give up when he doesn't let go. "And this time, I don't have to climb through the window or have a gun aimed at me."

He laughs and drags me with him toward the window and shuts it from the outside, and then he continues to drag me around to the front of the house. He lets us inside, and Bruce starts to take off down the hall but stops when Tyler growls, "Bruce, bed."

With a longing look in the direction he was going, Bruce moves to a dog bed placed next to the fireplace in the living room and sits down. "Now, let's see if we can get your cat."

"Can I have my hand back?" I ask, liking his firm hold a little too much, and his eyes drop to my hand still held in his.

"For now," he answers, looking at me, and my stomach dips as he finally releases my hand.

I ball it into a fist at my side and then sweep my other hand out toward his back hall. "After you."

He leads the way and stops at a closed door. He turns the handle, and Mouse—never one to miss an opportunity to frustrate me—runs past us as soon as it's cracked open. Thankfully, there's no way for him to get outside. Still, I don't know if Bruce will eat him for a snack, so I take off after him. When I reach the living room, I scan for his hiding place, then shake my head at him when I see he's next to Bruce on the dog bed.

"You're in so much trouble, mister." I pick him up, and he hisses and tries to get free. I tighten my hold, then look at Tyler. "Sorry."

"For what?"

My nose scrunches up. "I don't know. I just feel like I need to apologize."

He grins and comes toward me, then plucks Mouse from my hands. "I'll walk you two back to your place."

"You don't have to do that."

"I think I do," he counters, heading for the door, and then he stops to look at Bruce, who's at my side. "Stay, bud. I'll be back."

Bruce sits, and I give him a quick rubdown before Tyler opens the door and leads us out. When we reach my porch, I try to take Mouse, but Tyler just shakes his head, so with a sigh I let us inside. When I see and smell smoke filling the air, I rush to the kitchen and pull the hot pan off the stove. I drop the pan into the sink and turn on the water over the now-blackened meat.

"Was that your dinner?" Tyler asks, looking over my shoulder and still holding Mouse.

"It was." I sigh, looking back at the pan as steam rises off it.

"Get your coat."

"What?" I glance at him in confusion.

"Get your coat. I haven't eaten dinner yet. We'll go out."

My stomach flips and growls. I shake my head and open my mouth, but before I can get anything out, he cuts me off.

"Don't try to feed me some lame excuse of why you can't go. Just get your jacket on."

I look into his eyes, then down at the pan. I'm hungry, but am I hungry enough to go out with him?

"Leah, we're neighbors. You can't avoid me forever." He drops Mouse to the floor, and he runs off, but not before glaring at me over his shoulder.

"I haven't been avoiding you."

"Babe." He grins. "Seen you watching me more than once out the window, yet you avoid coming outside when I'm in my yard. And just today, when I was getting out of my truck, you made sure to look away before you could catch my eye."

Oh my God. My face heats. "I've never watched you when you're outside in your yard."

"Whatever, just get your jacket so we can go."

"I—"

"Fuck it, you don't need a jacket." He grabs my hand and starts to pull me toward the front door, and my heart begins to pound like crazy against my rib cage.

When his hand lands on the handle, I squeak, "Fine. Fine! Okay, let me get my coat."

He releases me, and I take a step away from him, keeping my eyes locked on his.

"Maybe—" I start, but I stop when he takes a step toward me. I turn quickly and go to the coat closet and pull out my jean jacket. I put it on and turn to face him. "Happy now?"

He doesn't answer me; he just holds the door open for me to exit ahead of him. "Sheesh," I huff, and I keep on huffing as he puts me in his truck and takes me to dinner.

Suggestion 3

Do Not Kiss Him

LEAH

"Hey, sugar," Grandma greets me as soon as she steps into the salon. At seventy-eight, my grandma still has it going on. She doesn't have many wrinkles on her face—probably from the Botox she will never admit she gets. Her thick silver hair is styled in a bob that accentuates her oval-shaped face and big blue eyes. She's tan from getting sprayed in a booth down the street every other week, and her clothes are always stylish. Today she's wearing simple black boots, black jeans, and a tight-fitting black blouse that is undone to show a hint of cleavage. She doesn't look much older than my mom, who's knocking on sixty's door, though my mom looks younger than her age too.

"Hey, Grams." I lean my head back so she can kiss my cheek. "I didn't think you were coming in for a while."

"Maria called, asked if I could fit her in this morning. She decided to give herself bangs last night." She laughs while she walks across the salon to her station and puts her purse in the bottom drawer. With just four stations, ours is one of the smaller salons in town. We are also one of the busiest, with people walking in off the street and a long list of standing clients.

The place has not changed in years and could do with some updating, but that would mean shutting the salon down for renovations, and I don't ever see that happening. We would probably be chased through the streets with pitchforks if we told our clients we were closing for weeks and they had to wait to get their hair done. That's why the floors are still the same black-and-white checkered tile they've always been, and the stations look like something from the sixties; even the pink leather chairs have been there since the salon opened. My grandmother and mom and I have made it a point to keep things clean and in good condition, so the place at least doesn't look run down.

"So how was your night?"

At her question, I spin in my chair to face the mirror so I don't have to look at her when I answer. Last night, dinner with Tyler was . . . well, it was really good. We went to a local diner and ate at the bar because the place was packed. I found out over hamburgers and fries that Tyler had moved here from Tennessee after a friend of his who owns a construction company had offered him a job as a foreman.

He told me a little bit about his family, that his mom and dad are still married and that he has a sister and niece who live in Montana. I told him about going to school for nursing but then going back to school to get my cosmetology license and a little about my parents, brothers, and grandma. I also learned that he's even more determined than I am when he wants something. He flat out refused to let me pay for dinner, and it wasn't until he pointed out that people were watching us argue that I gave up the fight and let him pay.

After that, he drove us back home, and I didn't expect it, but he walked me to my door and made sure I was inside before he left. I had to remind myself all night that it hadn't been a date, that it had just been two neighbors having a meal and talking. But still, there was no denying I was attracted to him and enjoyed spending time with him. *Crap.*

"Sugar," Grams calls, and I focus on the mirror and find her standing behind me. "What's going on? You were miles away."

"Sorry." I shake away my thoughts.

"Are you thinking about your date tonight?" she asks, and my eyes widen.

Crap. How the heck did I forget about my date with Charles tonight? Charles and I dated for two years in high school. We were as serious as sixteen-year-olds could be and broke up right before we graduated since we were going to different colleges. I heard after our breakup that he had cheated on me numerous times, but I never told anyone except for my best friend, Chrissie. I didn't even confront him; I just wrote him out of my life. I was dating Chris when he moved back to town a few years ago, and after he and I broke up, Charles started to ask me out. I always made up reasons to say no until he asked me out to dinner a little over a week ago while I was at lunch with my mother. She, of course, thought it was a great idea for me to go out with him, because she'd always liked him, and as with a lot of women in town, she thought he was a catch because he was young, attractive, and a lawyer. What those women don't know is he's also still a player, and I have no desire to be played with. I didn't want to go, but with my mom staring at me from across the table with hope in her eyes, I felt like I didn't have a choice. Now that date is tonight.

Double crap.

"Yeah, just trying to think of what I'll wear," I lie.

"It doesn't matter what you wear. You look beautiful in anything you put on."

"Mmm-hmm," I half agree, wondering if there's a way to get out of tonight.

"Where's he taking you again?"

"The Wheelhouse, I think." I pick up my phone and scroll through my texts until I find the message he sent me last week.

"That's a nice place. I say a dress. Maybe that black one you have with the lace long sleeves and mock turtleneck."

"Yeah, maybe," I agree, reading the message from him—the one and only text he sent, telling me where we were going to dinner and what time he would pick me up at my house.

"Why are you frowning?" Grams questions, and I toss my phone to the top of my station.

"No reason."

"You seem annoyed," she points out as the bell over the door rings, saving me from further questions.

Maria rushes in with the hair over her eyes cut at an odd angle. "Help!" she cries as soon as she spots Grams.

"Oh, honey, what were you thinking?" Grams asks, taking Maria's hand and leading her over to her chair.

Maria plops down with a huff and tosses her bag on the top of Grams's station. "I wasn't thinking. I was sucked into the vortex of YouTube, where some girl convinced me that I could give myself bangs," she says, and I giggle. She's not the first to come into the salon having taken scissors to her hair, then regretted it afterward.

"No one can cut their own bangs," Grams informs her while tossing a cape around her shoulders. "Everyone messes them up when they try to do it themselves."

"I know that now, but can you fix it?" Maria asks, looking worriedly at her reflection.

"Thankfully, you didn't cut too much, so I should be able to."

"Thank God," Maria sighs in relief.

I spin my chair around so I can watch Grams go to work doing what she does best, and twenty minutes later, Maria leaves with even bangs and a smile on her face. Five minutes after she's gone, my first client of the day shows up, and the rest of the day is filled with client after client, giving me no time to think about my impending date with Charles.

I check out my reflection in the mirror while turning from side to side. My black mock turtleneck dress hits me just above the knees and fits me like a second skin. The long lace sleeves make the simple dress sexy, but the black leather high-heeled booties slouched around my ankles give the outfit a somewhat casual look. My long brown hair is pulled back away from my face with a clip, and my makeup is light, just some mascara, blush, bronzer, and lip gloss.

After getting home from working on my feet all day, I'm not in the mood to go out, but Charles sent a text this afternoon confirming he would be at my house tonight to pick me up, and I stupidly didn't take that opportunity to back out of the date. When the bell rings, I take one last look at myself and grab my clutch off the bed. I make my way across the living room, and as soon as I open the door, I start to tell Charles I'll just be a minute after I change out my bag, but it's not Charles. It's Tyler—Tyler wearing a pair of workman boots, dark jeans, and a long-sleeve black shirt that's plastered over every ridge and valley of his torso.

His eyes roam over me from my hair to my heels, and his look feels like a physical caress. When his blue eyes meet mine from under the brim of his black baseball cap, I shift uncomfortably from his gaze.

"Is everything okay?" I prompt when he says nothing.

"Are you going out?"

I want to tell him no for some reason, but then Charles pulls into my driveway in his BMW. "Yes. Did you need something?"

His attention comes back to me at my question.

"I didn't know you had a boyfriend." His statement whips out like an accusation, and my hand tightens on the door.

"I don't," I say; then my eyes move to where Bruce is standing on my porch near the steps, growling at Charles, who is now coming up my walk.

"Leah," Charles calls with fear in his voice, his eyes locked on Bruce.

"Hey, Charles, he's not going to hurt you," I tell him; then I look at Tyler. "Call Bruce off."

His jaw jumps as he orders, "Bruce, heel," without taking his eyes off mine.

"I think I'll wait in my car. Just come down when you're ready, and we can go," Charles says, backing away from Bruce, who sits down in the middle of the porch.

"I'll be right there," I agree, giving him a reassuring smile.

"Okay, sweetheart." He looks between Tyler and me before turning around and getting back in his car.

"Sweetheart?" Tyler shakes his head.

"If you don't need anything . . . ," I start, but I stop when he forces me back into my house, using his big body to do it. When he has me inside, he closes the door and crosses his arms over his chest.

"What kind of guy just gets in his car when the woman he's going on a date with is talking to another man he doesn't know?"

That's a good question, but since I don't have an answer, I keep my mouth closed.

"Why the fuck are you going out with a tool like him, Leah?"

"First," I hiss, getting pissed that he's asking me the same questions I've been asking myself all day, "you have no right to barge into my house. And second, who I date or why I'm dating them is not your business." I turn away from him and pick up my purse. I quickly and angrily transfer my wallet and cell phone into my clutch, then grab my coat and put it on, tying the waist. "If you don't mind, I need to leave, so please get out of my way."

His jaw clenches, and I can see he wants to say more, but he smartly keeps his mouth shut before heading outside. With my heart pounding and frustration twisting my gut, I walk out behind him and lock up my house. Tyler is halfway between his house and mine when I turn around, but Bruce is still sitting on my porch at the top of the stairs.

"Be a good boy and go home with your dad." I rub the top of his head, and he stands. "Go on," I order as I head down the stairs. I walk to the passenger-side door of Charles's car and grit my teeth when he doesn't even get out to open it for me. When I slide into the seat and slam the door, he starts to back out of the driveway before I even have my seat belt on.

"Who's that guy?"

I glance at him. Now he wants to know?

"My neighbor," I answer as he stops at a red light.

He smiles tightly; then his eyes roam my face. "You look good, Leah."

"Thank you." He looks good, too, and he's the kind of guy who knows he does. With his blond hair, golden tan, and eyes the color of the ocean, he is the definition of the all-American guy. He couldn't be more opposite of Tyler if he tried.

When my cell phone buzzes in my purse tucked on my lap, I pull it out. My eyes get squinty when I read the message on the screen.

Tyler: Do not kiss him.

Who does he think he is?

"Everything okay?" Charles asks as I type back quickly.

Me: You have no say in that.

"Yep, everything is good. Just my grandmother asking me a question about an order I placed for the salon." I turn the ringer off so I'm not tempted to look at it again if he messages back, and I tuck my cell away.

"Have you thought about giving up the hair business and going back to the real world?"

Annoyance makes my neck tight, but I still keep my voice even as I ask, "The real world?"

"You know what I mean." I do, and that pisses me off. "You were a nurse, and now you do hair."

"Mmm-hmm." I want to tell him that last year I made close to a hundred grand just doing hair, and I was able to buy my house—something I probably would not have been able to do working as a nurse. But instead, I say nothing.

"Don't be mad. I was just curious." He touches my leg, and I instantly feel like I'm doing something wrong.

"I'm not mad." I cross my legs so his hand is forced to fall away. "Since I got my cosmetology license, friends and family have asked me the same thing. I'm used to the question." *I'm just annoyed you asked me with such a self-righteous tone,* I leave out. "How's work in the real world going for you?"

"Busy. Have you seen our newest commercial?"

"Yeah." I did see it, or one of many just like it, constantly playing on all the local stations. His dad owns one of the bigger injury law firms around, and Charles, who followed in his daddy's footsteps, works for his firm. The commercials are all the same—him or his dad giving a check to someone in a hospital bed or a wheelchair.

When we reach the restaurant, we get out of his car and head inside. The interior is dimly lit, and with just a few tables and booths covered in white tablecloths, it's one of the few places in town where you need a reservation. I've been here before with my family to celebrate. The food is good, but I still prefer eating a hamburger and fries while sitting at a bar to this.

When we reach our table, I slip off my coat and place it on the back of my chair, then take a seat as Charles does the same. After the waitress comes to take our drink orders, I pick up my menu. "Order anything you want," Charles says, and I smile, thinking I was going to do that anyway.

By the time our dinner arrives, I'm tempted to go to the bathroom and escape out the window. Charles has been a gentleman, like he always was, but all night he has not stopped talking about himself, the people he knows, and the places he's been. At this point, I wouldn't be surprised if he pulled out his bank account and credit score to show me how well he's doing financially.

"So when the mayor asked if I'd come to his house for dinner, I, of course, had to say yes."

"Of course," I agree. I pick up my wineglass and take a sip, when I really just want to chug it like it's a two-dollar beer.

"Would you like to come?"

Coughing and choking on wine, I pick up my napkin and cover my mouth. Once I can breathe again, I shake my head. "I'm busy then, but thanks."

He frowns. "I haven't even told you when it is."

Oh, oops.

"Sorry, I thought you mentioned it was next weekend."

His face falls. "I must have. It's next Saturday."

Thank goodness.

"Yeah, I thought that's what you said." I give him what I hope is a somber smile. "Unfortunately, I'm babysitting my brother's two little ones for the weekend." It's not a lie. I told my brother a few weeks ago that I'd watch my nephews, Owen and Isaac, so he could take his wife away for a night. I don't mind. My nephews, who are five and seven, are adorable and pretty easy to keep happy. Plus, they love spending time with their cool aunt.

"Maybe your mom can watch them for a few hours while you come with me?" he suggests.

My mom would take them for a few hours if I asked her to, especially for me to go out with Charles again, but I'm not going to ask her.

"She's busy. I'm sorry; maybe another time."

"Yeah, though I'm not sure when I'll be invited to the mayor's house for dinner again." He picks his fork and knife back up and cuts into his steak, and I return to my salmon. When the check arrives after we've finished eating, he pays, making a production of doing it, and I almost roll my eyes but instead thank him for buying me dinner.

"Do you feel up to coming back to my place for a drink?" he asks as he pulls out of the parking lot of the restaurant.

Why do we not have the advanced technology of teleportation yet? "I have to be up early to open the salon. I'm sorry."

"I understand work." He glances at me. "I'd like to take you out again. Tonight was nice."

"Dinner was nice." Dinner *was* nice. Sitting across from *him* during dinner—not so much. "We'll have to see if our schedules mesh."

"Just text me. I'll let you know if I'm available when you are, and we'll work it out."

I don't agree or disagree, because I see my house come into view and a shadow on my porch in the shape of Bruce.

"Is that your neighbor's dog?" Charles asks as he pulls in to park in my driveway.

"Yeah."

"You should call animal control. No dog his size should be left unleashed to wander a family neighborhood."

"He's harmless."

"He didn't sound harmless when he was barking at me earlier."

I ignore his statement and unhook my belt. "Thank you again for dinner."

When I open my door, he grabs my wrist, stopping me before I can get out. "I would walk you up and kiss you good night at your door. I hope you understand why I'm not going to do that," he says, tightening his grasp and pulling me closer to him. When I see his eyes drop to my mouth, I lean my head back and smile.

"It's okay. I can walk myself." I pull free from his hold, put one foot out of the car, then the other, and Bruce appears at my side. "Hey, big guy." I rub the top of his head after I've slammed the car door closed, and Charles rolls down the window.

"Text me your schedule," he demands before he gives me a smug smile, then rolls the window up and backs out of the driveway. I watch him go with my hand on the top of Bruce's head, then look down at him. "What are you doing out so late?"

"He's been waiting for you to get home."

I spin around at the sound of Tyler's voice and see him standing at the end of my sidewalk.

"He refused to leave your porch, and I wasn't about to carry him home."

"And you, why are you here?"

"You didn't kiss him." It's a statement, not a question, and I lift my chin.

"You don't know that. I could have been making out with him the entire time I was gone."

"If that's the case, he was doing it wrong, because you don't look like you've been kissed." The way he's looking at me makes me want to know what I would look like after kissing him.

"Do you need me to walk Bruce to your house for you?"

"Bruce is fine. Why didn't you answer my last text?" he asks as I head up the walkway past him to my front porch.

"I was on a date. It's rude to text when you're on a date."

"It's rude to ignore messages from your neighbors."

"When your neighbor is annoying, it's not." I pull out my house key when I reach my front door and put it in the lock. I don't open it; I turn to face Tyler, who leans in next to me. "Are you not going home?"

"Do you have any beer?"

I should tell him no and then tell him to go home, but there's something about him that I like, even if he does exasperate me at the same time.

"Is that your way of asking if you can come in for a drink?" He shrugs. I pull in a breath, then let it out. "Fine, but the second you start to get on my nerves, I'm kicking you out."

"I'll be on my best behavior."

"I'm sure." I push open the door, and Bruce follows us inside. After I shut the door, I slip off my coat and look around for Mouse, but he's nowhere in sight. "Bruce," I call, and he comes toward me with his body shaking. "Do not eat my cat." I bend over his big dog body and rub him down, then stand and look at his owner. "Beer's in the fridge. I'm going to go change."

"You look beautiful tonight, Leah." Caught off guard by the compliment, I stare at him, unblinking. "Really beautiful," he says before he turns away. Suddenly, my lungs feel funny, and my chest feels warm. "Go change. I'll make sure Bruce doesn't eat Mouse if he comes out of hiding," he calls from the kitchen, where he disappears.

I rush to my bedroom and close the door and change into a pair of sweatpants and a sweatshirt and some slippers. When I reach the kitchen, Tyler's holding Mouse against his chest with one hand and a beer in the other. Mouse, who is not normally okay with being held, is rubbing his head against Tyler's jaw, and even from across the room, I can hear him purring.

"Did he come out of hiding, or did you find him somewhere?" I ask, going to the fridge to grab a bottle of wine.

"He was on top of the fridge. He jumped down at me when I opened the door."

"He's done that to me at night when I've come in here to get water. The first time it happened, I almost wet myself." I smile when he laughs. I grab a wineglass from one of the glass-inlaid cabinets and pour myself half a glass, taking a sip as I walk the bottle back to the fridge.

"Do you have work tomorrow?"

"Yeah, tomorrow is my day to open the shop. My mom, my grandma, and I take turns."

"What time do you have to be there?"

"Seven thirty. Saturdays start early and end late for me. Are you working tomorrow?" I lean against the counter across the kitchen from him.

"Yeah, the job I'm on now is running six days a week. The only reason it's not seven is because it's a church, and the pastor doesn't want us messing up his sermon on Sundays."

"That makes sense."

"Do you work Sunday?" he asks, setting Mouse on top of my kitchen table before standing next to me and leaning back against the counter while he takes a pull from his beer.

I watch his Adam's apple bob as he swallows, then answer his question. "We're closed on Sundays. We used to be open, but most of our clients go to church, so it's more cost efficient to close down the shop."

"If you're not busy, you wanna help me paint my kitchen Sunday?"

Normally I'd think we don't know each other well enough for me to help him with something like that, but we did have a meal together, and I do find it easy to be around him. "I'm not very good at anything handy, so I don't know how helpful I'd be."

His eyes wander over me. "I'm sure I'll find some way to use you."

My nipples tingle, along with the area between my legs. His crass comment shouldn't turn me on, but it does.

"So what do you say?"

"Sure," I agree, and he smiles, taking another drink from his beer.

"So who's the guy in the BMW?"

How did I know this was coming? "Just a guy."

"You got dressed up to go out to dinner with him," he points out.

"He was taking me to a nice restaurant. I wasn't going to wear jeans and combat boots." I sip my wine, then give him what he's obviously searching for. "His name is Charles; we dated for a couple years when we were in high school. He's a lawyer. I normally wouldn't have agreed to dinner with him, but he asked me out in front of my mom, and my mom thinks he's a catch, so I agreed to a date. I went, I found out what I already knew—I'm not interested at all—and I won't be seeing him again."

"Good." He takes another pull from his beer.

"I won't be seeing him again because I don't want to, not because you don't want me to."

"Whatever. As long as you're not seeing him again, I don't give a fuck what your reasons are."

"Remember when I said I'd kick you out if you aggravated me?"

He smirks, and I swear there's something about that confident look that makes me want to throw myself against him and pull his mouth down to mine. My heart speeds up, and my stomach actually tugs in his direction, like it's trying to get me to move toward him. I don't do it, but I swear, from the look he gives me, he knows I want to.

Crap.

Suggestion 4

TELL HIM THE TRUTH

LEAH

With my feet aching, I get out of my car and head into my house while the garage door closes behind me. Once inside, I kick off my heels near the door to the garage and wander barefoot down the hall toward my bedroom.

Saturdays at the salon are no joke. I was busy from the moment I opened the doors at eight until my last client left at seven. All I want to do is put on some comfortable clothes, find something to eat, and sit on my couch with my feet up. When I reach my bedroom, I strip out of my top and jeans and put on a pair of leggings and one of my old baggy T-shirts.

I go to the kitchen and flip on the light, and Mouse, who's on top of the upper cabinets, meows at me. "I know; I'm getting your dinner first." I grab a pack of his wet cat food and dump it in his bowl, then go in search of something to make for myself. Hearing an odd scraping sound coming from the front room, I head in that direction, and the scraping sound stops. I really hope I don't have mice. I swear I will lose it if I do. The noise comes back, and I realize it's coming from the front door. I unhook the lock, pull it open, and smile when I see Bruce.

"Hey, big guy." I rub the top of his head and scratch behind his ears. I let him inside and go in search of my phone so I can let Tyler know I have his dog. Last evening, Tyler stayed until he finished his beer, and while he was here, Bruce and Mouse seemed to get along. There were a couple of times when Mouse went out of his way to try to annoy him, but Bruce ignored him for the most part. Okay, he chased him through the house when he was done being pestered, but he didn't bite him. Then again, he didn't catch him either.

I finally find my phone and send Tyler a text before I go back to the kitchen with Bruce on my heels. I grab a big bowl, one of the ones I use when I bake, because a cereal bowl just isn't going to cut it. I dump half a box of Fruity Pebbles in it, then top it off with milk. I take my bowl of cereal to the living room and turn on the TV. Once I'm seated, I sigh as I put my feet up on the coffee table.

Bruce lies at my feet as I flip through channels. I eventually find something worth watching and dig into my dinner. Halfway through an episode of *The Real Housewives*, the doorbell rings, so I reluctantly get off the couch. Taking my bowl with me, I step over Bruce, who doesn't get up. When I pull the door open, Tyler smiles at me, then frowns down at my meal.

"Is that your dinner?"

"Yes." I leave him to close the door, and I step over Bruce again, taking a seat and putting my feet back up.

"Long day?" he asks.

"The longest," I respond before filling my mouth with soggy fruity goodness.

He takes a seat next to me so close that his thigh brushes mine, then rests his arm on the back of the couch over my shoulders. "My dog's abandoned me." At his comment, I glance at him and see he's looking at Bruce lying under my outstretched legs. "Since I got home from work, I only saw him long enough to feed him. Right after that, he pounded on the door until I let him outside, and then he came right over here to camp out on your porch."

"He's sweet and obviously has good taste in women."

"I think he and I might have that in common." He holds my gaze, and my belly dips. Seriously, he knows how to give a girl butterflies with just a few words.

"How was your day?" I look away from him and scoop up another spoonful of cereal, hoping if I keep my mouth busy, I won't be tempted to use it on him.

"Good. Busy. The job's half-done, so it won't be much longer until we move on to another project."

"Do you know what your next project is?"

"We just won a bid to start renovations on one of the hotels by the beach. We're doing a complete overhaul of all the rooms on the top two floors."

"Sounds fun." I bite my bottom lip when he starts to play with a piece of my hair.

"It's work." He slouches back on the couch, obviously making himself more comfortable, and then lifts his boots to my coffee table. His boots are huge, especially compared to my bare feet. I wonder if it's true what they say about shoe size and the size of other stuff. "Is that any good?"

I look at him with my mouth full and raise a brow as I chew and swallow. "Did you just ask if Fruity Pebbles is any good? Have you ever had it?"

"I haven't eaten cereal since I was a kid. The only kind my ma ever bought for us was Cheerios, and not the real kind—the kind that comes in the family-size bag."

"Here." I lift a full spoon up toward him, and he looks down at it. "Don't be a chicken; just try it."

He leans forward, and his lips wrap around the spoon I'm holding, the sight way more erotic than it should be. He chews and swallows, shaking his head. "It's . . ."

"Delicious," I finish for him. "Do you want some more?"

"I'm good." He laughs. "I am worried that you're eating that for dinner."

"Why? It's fruit and dairy," I deadpan, and he laughs again.

"Whatever you say, gorgeous. Tomorrow I'll make you breakfast so your body has the fuel it needs before we get to work."

I haven't forgotten I'm spending the day with him tomorrow, pretending to help him paint his kitchen. I've been thinking about it all day today. I've been thinking about *him* all day today, actually. I really am starting to like him, even if he has the ability to annoy me like no one else I have ever met in my life.

"Will there be bacon?" I set my bowl on the coffee table, then lean back against the couch, looking at him.

"Is that your roundabout way of saying you want bacon?"

"Yep."

"Then I guess there will be bacon."

"Now I can't wait for breakfast." I smile at him when he grins. "I do have to leave around four, or maybe a little earlier, so I can shower and change to get to my parents' place for Sunday dinner."

"Sunday dinner?"

"Yeah, do you want to come?" *Crap, why the heck did I just ask him that?* I didn't mean to. It just came out before I could stop it. "I mean . . ."

"Sure," he agrees.

"Oh . . . okay. Awesome." I bite the inside of my cheek. My mom is going to flip her lid—not in a bad way. She's going to be so happy I'm bringing a man with me that she will probably start knitting baby booties. Not that she knits. She'll probably just order some off Amazon for free two-day delivery.

My parents were not always concerned about my love life, or lack thereof. When I was in my twenties, they told me that I didn't need to look for a serious relationship, that I should focus on myself and experience as much life as possible. The day I turned thirty, that all changed. Even my dad, who is protective of his only girl, thinks I need to find someone to settle down with. He's always giving me concerned looks when we have dinner with my two brothers, who both got married and had kids before the age of thirty.

"You don't want me to go?" He tugs that piece of hair he hasn't stopped playing with, and I turn my head.

"It's not that. I just . . . well, I've never invited someone to Sunday dinner. I mean, I have, but not a guy. My parents and brothers might assume . . ." I look away at his smirk, and my face gets warm. "It's just . . ." I blow out a breath. "You know how parents and siblings are."

"We're friends. I'm new in town, and we're neighbors."

"Right," I agree, even though it's a little disappointing to think he's not interested in me and that the comments he's made haven't been a lead-up to something more—that something more being him fricking kissing me. But maybe that's just him . . . maybe he flirts with everyone.

"I don't have to come if you're going to be uncomfortable."

I turn to look at him once more. "You're right. We're just friends and neighbors; it won't be a big deal."

"Hmm."

Okay, what does that mean? Never mind. I don't want to know. I focus on the TV and not so much on him playing with my hair or sitting so close that the weight of him on my couch forces us even closer together.

"You should go to bed. You've yawned three times in as many minutes," he tells me.

"I need to know if Bethenny is going to tell Luann about her husband being with another woman," I say, keeping my eyes glued to the TV.

"I'm sure you can google it if you really need to know."

"True." I yawn again, and my eyes water.

"Come on." He stands, then pulls me up with him off the couch. "Walk me to the door, then go on to bed." He walks to the door and stops with his hand on the handle, then looks at Bruce, who hasn't gotten up. "Bud, come on. Time to go home."

"Come on, big guy." I pat my thighs, and he comes instantly, and I laugh as Tyler grumbles under his breath. "I'll see you tomorrow," I tell Bruce, hugging him around his furry neck, and then I stand and look at his dad. "When do you want me?"

His eyes change ever so slightly, and I swear he's going to say something dirty, but he doesn't. "Nine thirty or ten."

"Okay," I agree.

He touches his fingers to my cheek, then opens the door and steps out onto the porch. "Bruce, come," he calls when Bruce doesn't follow him. I giggle, and he shakes his head as I push Bruce outside with my hands on his rump. "See you in the morning, babe."

"Mmm-hmm." I watch him walk down the stairs and roll my eyes when he orders me into my house and to lock the door. I do what he asks, only because I want to, but I still watch him through the window as he and Bruce walk across the grass between his yard and mine and up to his front door. When he's inside, I go back to the TV and turn it off, then get in bed, where eventually I fall asleep thinking about the guy next door.

"That's a lot of tape," I point out as Tyler adds more and more blue tape to the edge of the backsplash where it meets the wall.

"You said yourself you aren't handy. I just want to make sure the backsplash and counters aren't ruined today."

"Wouldn't it have been smarter to put the backsplash and the counters in after you painted?" I check out the paint color he chose for the kitchen. The smoky-blue color will go great with the speckled gray, silver, and blue granite of the countertop and the glossy white tile for the backsplash, which has pieces of blue and gray glass mixed in.

"That was the plan, but the counters showed up, so I put them in, and then I couldn't stand looking at the yellow backsplash anymore, so I ripped it out and put in the new stuff."

"Wait, you did all this yourself?" I look around his kitchen, and I'm seriously impressed. The space is open all the way to the living room, and a large peninsula divides the two rooms. He has state-of-the-art appliances, a double fridge that I would never be able to keep stocked, an oven built into the wall, a microwave under the counter, and a five-burner gas range in the peninsula. This morning he made me french toast, bacon, and eggs on a cast-iron griddle after I showed up, and we ate while sitting at the island in his kitchen. I don't know if it was his cooking or just being in his company, but it was the best breakfast I've ever eaten.

"Baby, I'm a contractor. It's my job to remodel shit. I'm not going to pay someone else to do work I can do myself."

"Okay, but it's still impressive," I mutter, and he smiles at me as he adds a sheet of plastic and even more blue tape to the backsplash. "I'm starting to get offended by the amount of plastic and tape you're using."

He laughs, tossing back his head. He has a great laugh, rich and deep. I could listen to him laugh forever. I also like how he looks when he laughs, the way his big shoulders shake and his eyes light up. Frick, I just really like him.

"Just being safe. Anyway, I'm done." He rips off the tape and tosses the roll to the counter. "Are you ready to paint?"

"I guess." I shrug.

"Do you wanna borrow a shirt?" I look down at my old T-shirt, the same one I had on last night when he came over, and shake my head. "Then let's get to work." He comes over to where I'm standing and takes the can of paint from me. He then pries it open, mixes it, and dumps some into a painting tray. When he's done, he hands me a small angled brush. "We'll start on the edges. You take the bottom, and I'll take the top. Once we get them all done, we'll add another coat; then I'll hit the rest with the roller to finish it out."

"Sounds easy enough, and I'm a pro at highlights, so this can't be much different."

"Not sure coloring someone's hair and painting a wall are the same, but I guess we'll find out." He grins. I grin back, then watch what he does before I start on the other side of the kitchen. "Did you let your family know I'm coming to dinner?"

I bite my lip hard at the reminder he's coming to my parents' house with me this evening. "Not yet, but I'll let my mom know after we're done here."

"I don't want to be an inconvenience."

I stop painting so I can turn to look at him. "She cooks for an army. I always end up taking home leftovers. Plus, she loves feeding people. She'll be happy to have another person to push food on."

"Your mom sounds like my mom. Being southern, she thinks of food as love."

"It kind of is, isn't it?" I go back to painting. "My parents' kitchen was where we congregated when I was growing up. It was where we talked, where we spent time together, even when we were all busy doing our own thing. It's where we got advice when we had a problem, or just spent time laughing. Most of our time together as a family was spent over a meal or while preparing one."

"I guess you're right."

"I'm always right," I say smugly.

"You're a woman, so I guess you probably think that's true." Even though I'm not looking at him, I can hear the smile in his voice.

"Word of advice: you might not want to annoy me when I have a paintbrush in my hand," I warn, and he chuckles.

"Just speaking from experience. I have a mom and a sister who are always right, even when they aren't."

"Whatever," I mumble.

We're both silent while we work, and I'm just about to ask him to turn on the radio when he asks, "What are your plans next Sunday?"

I pause to put more paint on my brush and look at him. "I'm off, but I have my nephews for the weekend. We'll probably spend most of the time playing video games and eating all the junk food their parents won't let them have but I do." He raises a brow. "Don't judge me. I'm trying to keep the title of the cool aunt."

"I see."

"Anyway, my oldest nephew, Owen, is seven, and he's obsessed with anything to do with the ocean, so I might take him and his brother, Isaac, to the aquarium on Sunday. You're more than welcome to join us." Crap, there goes my mouth again, using words before asking me if they're okay to come out. "I mean, if you don't have plans already."

"No plans—count me in."

"Cool, it's a date. I mean, we've got plans."

He starts to laugh, and I have the urge to flick paint at him. I don't, because so far I haven't made a mess and I'm really trying to be neat.

"Can I ask something?" He breaks the silence that's settled between us once more.

"Sure." I shrug.

"Why the fuck don't you have a man?"

"Why don't you? I mean, a girlfriend." My stomach drops suddenly. "Unless you do."

"I don't." The statement is firm. "As to why not, I just hadn't found anyone worth pursuing." Should I read into him saying *hadn't* instead of *haven't*? No, I probably shouldn't. "Now you."

"Same. Well, kinda, anyway. I don't want to chase anyone. I've done that before, and it hasn't worked out, and I don't want to keep someone who doesn't want to be kept. Nowadays, it feels like the men

I've met don't actually know what they want. I'm thirty-three. I'm not saying I'm old, but I'm over the game playing and mixed messages. I'd rather be single than deal with all the confusion that comes along with a relationship."

"I get that," he says, and since I'm not looking at him, I can't read his expression.

We paint and chat, and before I know it, my part of the job is done, and I didn't get paint anywhere I wasn't supposed to. While he uses the roller brush to finish the job, I go into the living room and sit on the couch with Bruce.

"It looks good." I stand to survey the room while he washes the paintbrushes.

He looks around. "You did good. I might ask you to help me out with my bathroom next."

"Will there be french toast?"

"I'll make you french toast anytime you want it."

I don't have a comeback or want to get my hopes up, so I look at the clock on the front of the oven. "Since we're done, I'm going to head home to go shower. I'll be back here after I'm ready, if that works for you."

"I'll walk you over."

"I can make it across our yards without an escort." I roll my eyes at him.

"Yeah, but I'm still going with you," he says, walking to where I'm now giving Bruce a head rub. He takes my hand and leads me from his house, across our lawns, up my porch, to my front door. I let myself in, and he does the whole fingers-to-the-cheek thing I like a little too much before finally releasing his hold on me.

"I'll be back to get you. We'll take my truck."

"Sounds good. I'll see you then." I start to close the door, but Bruce, who followed us, tries to shove his way in using his large head and bulk to press against the door.

"Bud, you don't live here. Home," Tyler orders, and with a long, annoyed huff, Bruce stops trying to push inside. I laugh, and Tyler shakes his head, giving me a small grin before he heads off my porch. I go to my bedroom and dial my mom as I strip off my clothes. It rings and goes to voice mail, so I call her again as I start up the shower.

"Are you okay?" she asks worriedly as soon as she answers.

"I'm fine. I'm calling to let you know I'm bringing someone to dinner with me."

"Honey, you know Chrissie is always welcome. You don't have to call to tell me she's coming, especially not twice in a row. I thought something happened."

"It's not Chrissie. It's a guy," I announce, and there's silence on the other end of the phone, so I continue. "His name is Tyler. He just moved here from Tennessee." More silence. "Mom, are you still there?"

"I'm processing."

I tip my head back to look at the ceiling. "There's nothing to process; he's just a friend." A friend I want to kiss, but I'm not going to tell her that. "It's not a big deal. He just moved in next door. He's new in town and doesn't know anyone. I thought it would be nice for him to have a home-cooked meal."

That does it. When she speaks again, her voice is filled with understanding. "I'll see you two when you get here, honey. Love you."

"Love you too, Mom. See you then." I hang up and drop my phone on the vanity before I get in the shower.

I shampoo and condition my hair and shave everything, even though I have no reason to. I put on a robe and blow out my hair, then put on some light makeup. Dressed in a pair of deep-brown boots, dark jeans, and a sweater, I go to the kitchen to feed Mouse, who I haven't seen since this morning. As I'm dumping a can of wet food in his dish, he comes out of hiding.

"Are you still mad at me?" I pick him up and attempt to love on him as his claws come out and his tiny sharp teeth nip at my fingers.

Eventually, he wins the battle and gets away from me. He lands on his feet and goes to his dish, sniffing his food to make sure it's up to his standards before digging in. With time to kill, I call Chrissie to check on her since we haven't spoken in a few days. We've been best friends for years. She owns a bakery in town, which means, just like me, she's always busy working.

"I was just thinking about you," she says as a greeting, and I smile while walking into my living room.

"I feel like we haven't talked in forever." I take a seat on the couch.

"I know, right?" She groans. "We are both way too busy. Because we're old now, we need to plan a girls' night where we can drink and pretend the next day we won't be hungover."

"I'm not old. You might be old, but I'm not."

"We have the same birthday, so if I'm old, so are you." She laughs. "Anyway, how are things going with you? How was your date with Charles?"

"I'm good, busy, but then you know how that is. My date . . . well, it went about as well as I thought it would."

"So you won't be going out with him again?"

I snort. "You knew that was a onetime thing when I told you that I agreed to go out with him."

"Was it that bad?" she asks curiously. She knows about my history with Charles and is the only person who knows about the cheating rumors.

"It wasn't bad, but it wasn't good. He hasn't changed at all, and I don't know what I saw in him when we were young, even if I was just young and stupid. He didn't show any kind of chivalry, didn't open my door, didn't pull out my chair, didn't even wait for me to put on my seat belt before he started to drive. He talked about nothing but himself. Come to think of it, I don't even think he asked me one question about myself. Wait, that's not true. He asked if I've thought about giving up the whole hair gig and getting back to what he called the 'real world' of work."

"He didn't," she hisses.

"He did." I sigh. "Needless to say, I found out what I already knew: I won't be seeing him again."

"Where are all the good guys at?"

Tyler comes to mind, and I bite my lip before I tell her what I would only ever tell my best friend. "I've been spending time with my neighbor." I lean my head back.

"Your neighbor? Wait, the guy who pulled the gun on you?" She laughs, and I smile.

"Yeah, the same one. Chrissie, I swear he's . . . he's . . . well, he's awesome."

"So you're into him?"

"He's easy to be around and fun. I don't know if he's into me or not."

"So he hasn't made a move?"

"No, he's flirted a little but hasn't made a move." I hear the disappointment in my own voice. "Still, I like hanging out with him, so if I get a cool friend out of this in the end, I'm okay with that."

"Maybe he's just trying to take it slow and get to know you."

I snort. "Do guys even do that?"

"Not that I know of, but who knows? Maybe he's a different breed of man."

"Yeah, maybe," I agree.

"So what are you doing today?"

"I helped him paint his kitchen, and now he's coming with me to my parents' for dinner." The phone goes silent, and I pull it away to look at it. "Chrissie?"

"You're taking him to your parents' for dinner?" Her voice is filled with disbelief.

"We're friends, and like I said, he's cool."

"I'm coming!" she shouts.

"What?"

"I'm coming to dinner. I want to see this guy for myself."

I can tell she's excited about the idea.

I groan. "Chrissie—"

"You can't tell me I can't come. I'll just call your mom and ask her if it's okay that I join you guys."

"I'm not going to tell you that you can't come."

"Good. Besides, maybe I'll be able to give you an outside perspective about his feelings for you."

"I'm okay without that." I sigh. Dinner is going to be interesting.

Suggestion 5

BE HIS FRIEND

LEAH

"Thanks," I say as Tyler releases my hand and opens the passenger door for me. Once I'm seated, he slams it closed and walks around the front of the hood. I put on my seat belt while I check him out. His dark hair is still damp from his shower, but he didn't shave, so his jaw is covered in a layer of scruff that makes him seem hotter than his normal level of hot. The sweater he's wearing is one of those with a straight collar and a few buttons at his throat. It looks good on him, almost as good as his jeans. When he gets in behind the wheel, I give him directions to my parents' house, which is less than ten minutes away.

Needing something to do, I dig through my bag until I find my lip balm, then swipe some on. "I called my mom. She knows you're coming. My best friend, Chrissie, is also going to show up as soon as she closes down her shop."

"Her shop?"

"She owns the Sweet Spot. Have you been there?"

"The Sweet Spot?" He smirks at me.

"You're such a guy." I laugh. "It's a bakery. If you haven't been there, you need to make a point to go. She's good at what she does."

"I'll check it out," he agrees, and we fall into comfortable silence while Sam Hunt sings softly in the background.

When we reach my parents', I see we're the first ones here, which I'm kind of glad about. It's going to be weird enough without him meeting everyone at once. He walks over to my open door and takes my hand in his, holding it firmly even when I try to pull it away. I give up halfway up the walk with a loud sigh and swear I hear him laugh. I don't knock on my parents' door; I let us in.

My dad is sitting on the couch, and when he sees me, he stands, smiling at me as my mom comes into the room. My parents have been married since their twenties, and my dad has always managed a local grocery store. Dad's good looking for his age, with silver hair and bright-blue eyes. He runs every day to stay in shape and is tall—much taller than my mom, who's shorter than I am. My mom is beautiful, with long hair that she's always colored a deep reddish brown. Unlike me, she has fair skin, but we have the same blue eyes. Blue eyes that are looking at me with surprise. I ignore the look on Mom's face and introduce Tyler to my parents.

"Tyler, my dad, Gary, and my mom, Edith. Mom, Dad, this is Tyler."

"Nice to meet you, sir." Tyler lets me go to shake my dad's hand, and then he leans down to greet my mom with a kiss to her cheek and a softly spoken "Ma'am."

"Do you like football?" Dad asks, and I kind of zone out as they talk about their favorite teams and players.

"Why don't you come help me in the kitchen while the guys watch the game?" Mom suggests. It's not an actual suggestion. I know, because she wraps her hand tightly around my upper arm and starts to pull me with her. "Do you want a drink, Tyler?" Mom asks over her shoulder.

"I'm good for now. Thank you, though."

"Honey, you want anything?" she asks Dad.

"I'm okay." He doesn't pull his eyes from the TV.

"We'll be in the kitchen then." She marches me forward. I look back over my shoulder, and Tyler gives me a smile as he settles on the couch with my dad. "You did not tell me your new neighbor is *hot*," Mom whispers when we're out of earshot of the guys.

"I didn't think I needed to announce that during my phone call with you." I don't roll my eyes, because I'm not in the mood to be smacked upside the head—something I've seen my mom do to my brothers, even now that they are grown men.

"Honey, I'm your mom. I love your father to death, but you still need to give a woman some warning when you're going to show up for Sunday dinner with a man who is even hotter than Chris Hemsworth."

"No guy in real life is hotter than Chris Hemsworth," I scoff. Okay, Tyler is definitely up there with Chris on the hotness scale, but Chris as Thor totally knocks him out of the running. Seriously, Tyler doesn't even rank with Thor—no man alive ranks with Thor.

"Are you blind?" she asks, going to the oven and opening the door to check on the huge turkey she's cooking in the middle of October. Where did she find a turkey? I thought those were seasonal.

"Mom—"

"Just your neighbor," she mocks, shutting the door with her hip and raising a brow.

"He's my friend," I say, and she starts to laugh. "What's funny?"

"I cannot wait until your grandma gets here and gets a load of this guy."

"Grams is coming to dinner?" She doesn't normally come. She has a standing date with a "friend" every Sunday. And we call him her friend because the truth is just too gross to think about. *Gag.*

"She'll be here soon," she confirms.

"Chrissie is coming as well." I shrug. "The more the merrier."

She smiles at me, then asks softly, "Is he really just a friend?"

"You know I don't like disappointing you, but yes. I like him. He's easy to spend time with, but we're just friends."

Her expression fills with disappointment, then brightens. "He was holding your hand."

I don't have a good excuse for that. He is always holding my hand. Maybe he holds hands with everyone. Who the heck knows?

"What do you want me to help with?" I change the subject while looking around for something to do.

She's silent for a long moment before letting out a breath. "Nothing right now. When the boys get here, they can set the table. Dinner is already finished." She turns toward the fridge and pulls out a tray of deviled eggs.

"Is it Thanksgiving already?" I joke, and she gives me her don't-mess-with-me look. "Just asking."

I hear the commotion in the living room and slowly walk through the house. When I reach the hall, my brother Noah; his wife, Angie; and my nephews, Owen and Isaac, are taking off their coats and kicking off their shoes. Isaac sees me first and runs full speed in my direction, coming to a halt with his hands grasping my hips and his head tipped way back. "Dad told us on the way over here that we get to spend next weekend with you."

"You do." I slide my fingers through his soft brown hair and bend down to kiss his forehead. "We're going to eat so much junk food," I whisper, then lean back just in time to catch his grin. "It's our secret, though, so you have to keep it on the DL."

"What's the DL?" he whispers back, looking confused and completely adorable.

"The down low."

"Oh." His smile takes over his whole face. "I can do that."

"Good." I kiss the top of his head, then meet Owen's eyes. "Come here, dude."

He comes toward me much slower than his brother, because he's starting to become too cool for his aunt's hugs and kisses. I still wrap him up in a hug and lift him off the ground, even though he must weigh close to sixty pounds by now.

"I've missed you, kid." I pepper kisses on his cute face, laughing as he tries to dodge them. "Are you excited about next weekend?" I look into his happy eyes as he nods. "Good, I cannot wait to play *Fortnite* with you." I haven't ever played *Fortnite*, but I know it's the game all the kids are playing right now, so I bought it last week.

"Really?" he asks, sounding as excited as his brother did moments ago.

"Am I or am I not the best aunt in the whole entire world?"

"You are." He grins.

"Exactly, and I plan on keeping my spot." I kiss his forehead, then let him go.

"Buying love, sis?"

I look at Noah, who looks just like a brown-eyed version of our dad—tall, thin, and handsome.

"I'm just doing what needs to be done." I shrug, and he shakes his head and wraps his arms around me.

"You good?"

"Always." I smile as he kisses the top of my head.

"Who's the guy?" he asks quietly before he pulls away.

"A friend," I reply just as quietly, and then I go to Angie and kiss her cheek before I introduce Tyler to everyone.

"So are you her boyfriend?" Owen asks, looking between Tyler and me.

"No, he's just a friend." I don't look at Tyler or react to the hand that he places against my lower back. My eyes go to my mom's, and I see her smirking at me.

"Boys, I need you to set the table," Mom says, looking between Owen and Isaac, and they take off, probably wanting to get it done so they can go downstairs and play. She moves her gaze to my dad and brother. "I'm going to need you to drag up the spare table from the basement, along with a few extra chairs."

"On it." Dad stands and kisses the side of Mom's head.

"I'll help," Tyler adds, stepping away from me and following my dad and brother out of the room.

"Okay, you need to spill. Who is he, and where did you find him?" Angie asks, watching the guys disappear.

"He's my new neighbor and just a friend," I tell her on my way into the kitchen.

"Girls and guys cannot be friends," she informs me with authority.

"Yes, they can."

"Okay, a girl who looks like you and a guy who looks like him cannot be friends." She adjusts her stance, and I shake my head.

"I think my daughter is floating down the river Denial," Mom chimes in. "Did you see the hand-on-her-back thing?" she asks.

"I saw it." Angie nods.

"He was also holding her hand when they got here," Mom informs her.

"Hand-holding is not friendly." Angie looks at me.

"He always does it. He probably does it with everyone," I say, picking up a deviled egg and eating it. I'm starving, or maybe I'm finally finding a way to keep my mouth closed.

"Grandma," Isaac calls out from the doorway, saving me. "We're done. Can we go down to the basement and play video games until dinner?"

"Sure." She smiles at him; then her eyes come back to me.

Just as she's about to open her mouth, the front door opens, and Ben shouts through the house that he's here. I escape any further questions about Tyler and leave the kitchen. My brother Ben and his wife, Beth, both smile at me and laugh as Mia, my adorable four-year-old niece, screeches my name at the top of her lungs when she sees me.

"Hey, my beautiful girl." I scoop her up and kiss her cheeks and neck, listening to her giggle. "I've missed you so much." She doesn't reply with actual words, but she does wrap her arms around my neck and hug me back tightly. "How's my other niece doing?" I ask Beth, who is now five months pregnant.

She beams at me, then rests her hands on her swollen belly. "She's still cooking."

"You look beautiful." I lean over and kiss her cheek, then accept a one-armed hug from my brother.

"How are you?" Ben asks, while Beth takes Mia, who's asking for her grandma.

"I've been good, working lots. Same story, different day."

His eyes look over my head, and he frowns slightly. "Who's that?"

I turn and watch Tyler carry a set of chairs past the opening in the living room. "My friend Tyler. I'll introduce you in a sec. He's helping Dad and Noah bring up chairs from the basement. Grams is coming, and so is Chrissie. Mom needed more seating."

"You said friend. He's not your boyfriend?" He looks confused.

"He's just a friend. I don't know why that concept is so difficult for everyone to understand." I let out an annoyed sigh. I should have called everyone before dinner so I could explain the concept of "just a friend" to them.

"You've never had a guy friend before," he says, looking down at me. He looks a lot like Mom but is much taller with the same brown eyes as Noah and my exact hair color.

"Yes, I have."

"Okay, name one."

I try to think of one guy I've ever been just friends with, but I can't. Have I really never been friends with a guy before?

"Tyler."

"You're an idiot." He chuckles, then lowers his voice. "I'm just a little surprised. You've never brought anyone home for Sunday dinner besides Chrissie."

"I like him," I say, and he raises a brow. "He's easy to hang out with and fun to be around, but we really are just friends."

"All right, introduce me to this friend of yours." He slings his arm around my shoulders and leads me through the kitchen to the large dining room, where my dad, Tyler, and Noah are setting up chairs. I make introductions and then make my escape when the guys start to talk about guy stuff that I have no interest in.

I help my mom in the kitchen, then go down to play video games with the kids until Mom shouts down that dinner is ready. When I come upstairs, Grams is in the kitchen, and so is Chrissie. I hug both of them, then ask if they were introduced to Tyler. I don't even have to hear them say yes; I can tell by the glazed look in their eyes at the mention of his name that they have been.

Chaos ensues as we all sit down at the table and begin to prepare our plates. It's always loud and crazy, but this Sunday is more insane than usual. Different conversations are happening, the kids are being kids and shouting out what they want to eat so their parents can make their plates, and my mom is ordering everyone around. When we have our plates piled high, we sit and my dad says grace. That's the only minute of silence we have. As soon as he's done, everyone goes back to chatting.

I look at Tyler and watch him smile. "My family is a little crazy."

"I like them, and this reminds me of being home," he says, and my heart warms. I have never been far from home, and I don't know that I could adjust to moving out of the town I grew up in.

"I keep leaving you to fend for yourself," I point out, feeling a little guilty.

"I noticed." He laughs.

"Sorry about that."

"Don't be. I can take care of myself. Besides, I watched you blank out when your dad and I started talking about football. I get it's not your thing, hanging with the guys."

My nose scrunches up, and his eyes roam my face before he smiles. "For most of my childhood, we only had one TV. During football season, it was always on a game, and I never got to watch my shows. I won't say I hate football, but it doesn't interest me."

"I'll remember that." When he smiles again, my eyes drop to his mouth. Really, he has a great mouth and great lips. The top one has a nice curve to it, and the bottom is full.

Someone clears their throat, and I jerk my eyes off his mouth and look around, wondering if anyone saw me ogling my friend, who is really just that—my friend. Mom and Grams are both looking at me with the same exact look on their faces, a look that says they know I like this guy more than I'm admitting. I start to eat to keep my mouth busy.

Noah tells Tyler about the guys' upcoming fishing trip. "You should come with us," he says. "We normally head out Friday evening and get back Sunday afternoon." This is a trip my brothers and dad have gone on twice a year since I can remember. A trip my mom and I have never, ever been invited on. My brother inviting Tyler says just how much he likes him. Heck, everyone in my family likes him, and I think my best friend might even have a crush. I totally get it, because I have one too.

"Let me see if I can get the time off." Tyler leans back after he finishes his dessert. He places his arm on the back of my chair and twirls a piece of my hair around his finger. I can feel every eye at the table on me, but I don't look around. I ignore everyone and eat my apple pie with ice cream.

"Just let us know, and if you can't make it this time, we'll go again in the summer," Dad says.

Tyler responds with a "Sure." When a foot taps mine under the table, I look to my right at my best friend.

"I need to go to the restroom," she whispers.

"Okay," I whisper back.

"Don't you need to go to the restroom?" she asks, with wide eyes that glance between Tyler and me.

"You know we're at my parents' house and not a bar or restaurant, right?" I prompt quietly. She frowns at me, and I sigh. Apparently, I need to use the restroom. I get up with her and head down the hall. She drags me into the small dark room with her, and once she closes the door, she flips on the light.

"Friend?" she hisses, pulling down her pants and taking a seat on the toilet. Okay, so she really did need to use the bathroom. This isn't the first time we've used the bathroom at the same time, so I'm not even a little shocked right now. "That guy is not just your friend." She points at me, waving a piece of toilet paper around.

"He's just my friend." I turn on the water and wash my hands, needing something to do, and she joins me at the sink, looking in the mirror at me.

"Please tell me where I can find a friend like him, then." She rolls her eyes. "He hasn't stopped touching you and has made it perfectly clear to everyone what his intentions are."

Hope blooms in my chest. I know what I've felt every time he's touched me, but my judgment is clouded by my feelings for him. I do not want to assume he likes me. I don't want to think this is more than it is.

She scoffs, crossing her arms over her chest. "He's totally into you. And your family loves him."

"I'm happy everyone likes him, Chrissie, but until he makes a move or tells me that we're more, it is what it is. We're just friends."

"Le—" she starts, but I cut her off.

"I'm done playing games." I turn to face her. "I'm done making the moves in a relationship. I want a guy who knows what he wants. I want a guy who is willing to chase after me for once."

Her face softens with understanding. "I think you found him, Le."

I jerk my shoulders up, then let them fall. "I don't know what's going to happen, but I know I'm no longer going to settle. I don't want a guy who says one thing but means another. I don't want a man who thinks he's so perfect he doesn't have to put effort into a relationship."

"You're right." She bites her lip, glancing away quickly. "You deserve all of that. You deserve a guy who's willing to put himself out there, a guy who's willing to fight for you."

"So do you," I point out.

My best friend is gorgeous, with shoulder-length auburn hair, bright hazel eyes, and a body made up of tons of curves. She looks like a pinup model, and she's successful in her own right. She deserves to find someone to make her happy too.

She ignores my comment. "I still like him for you." She turns toward the mirror and adds, "He's really nice."

"He is really nice, which is why he's my friend." I grin at her, and she rolls her eyes. "Can we go back to the table now?"

"Sure." She opens the door and steps out before me.

When we get to the table, Tyler's eyes roam my face like he's assessing if I'm okay. I give him a reassuring smile, and he smiles back as I take a seat. After everyone finishes dessert, the kids go downstairs to play, the guys head to the living room to continue watching TV, and all the women go to the kitchen to clean up.

I know for a fact that my brothers do dishes at home and that my dad is usually the one to clean up after whatever meal my mom has cooked for him. Tonight, the women have taken over, because they all want to ask me about Tyler in private. I dodge question after question while we scrub plates, fill the dishwasher, and wipe down the counters. Even though I know they all love me, I wish they would just let things go.

I like Tyler. I like how he holds my hand, I like how he shows up without planning ahead, and I really like how he makes me feel. That said, I don't want to assume anything. I was with a man for two years, spending every evening at his house and waking in his bed thinking he might be my forever, while he was contemplating his commitment to me. I'm not willing to go through that again. I'm not willing to think this is something more when it's not.

If he likes me, then he's going to have to be the one to make the first move. He's going to have to be the one to step out on the ledge and put himself out there.

When we're finally done cleaning up the kitchen, we join the guys in the living room. We watch until the end of the game before calling it a night.

After hugs and kisses, Tyler walks me outside, holding my hand until we reach the passenger side of his truck, and then he places me inside. He drives me home and walks me to my door, touching my cheek with his fingertips before he steps back and lets me go, wishing me sweet dreams. Then, like usual, he orders me to lock up. After I've gotten into bed and Mouse has curled against my belly, I lie there awake for a long time, thinking about my life, thinking about Tyler, and thinking about what it would be like if he were actually the guy for me.

After I eventually fall asleep, I dream about him kissing me. The next morning when I wake up to bright light shining in on me through the curtains, I'm disappointed that our first kiss only came to me in a dream.

Suggestion 6

LET HIM TAKE THE LEAD

LEAH

Tyler: Pizza or Chinese tonight?

I read the text message from Tyler and smile as I type back, Chinese. We've had dinner together every night this week. We haven't once made plans, but like clockwork, he shows up not long after I get home, and we make dinner together. I guess he doesn't feel like cooking tonight, and really, I don't care what we eat, as long as I get my daily fix of him. My phone buzzes again, and I look at it.

Tyler: Let me know what you want and I'll see you at your place around six.

What I really say is *I want you*, but I don't. The sexual tension between us has been mounting, but like I told Chrissie, I'm not going to be the one to make the first move—no way, not this time. If he's interested in me, then he has to put his cards on the table. I've always been the one in my past relationships to make it clear I was interested in moving forward, instead of the guy taking the lead.

I text him my order, then get out of my chair and start to clean up my station. Once I'm done, I head for my mom, who's in the back of the salon.

"Everything okay?" Mom asks, and I lean my shoulder against the wall, watching her pull out foils from her client's hair.

"I don't have another client scheduled, so I'm going to leave a little early. I still need to get food for the boys, who are coming over tomorrow, and stop at the video game store."

"Don't you mean junk food?" She smirks.

"Of course. What other kind of food would I get for two growing boys I'm trying to bribe?"

She laughs, and her client laughs along with her.

"Okay, honey, are you doing anything fun tonight?" She knows Tyler and I have spent every evening together. She and Grams haven't let up on the questions since Sunday dinner, and I've been honest about what's happening. I've told them that nothing has changed between us, because nothing has. We are still just friends who enjoy each other's company.

"Tyler's bringing Chinese food." I shrug. "We'll probably watch a movie or something—I'm not sure."

"Well, have fun, and call me if you need my help with the boys over the weekend."

"I will. Love you." I push off the wall and kiss her cheek.

I get in my car and head to GameStop, then the grocery store. While I'm at the store, I get only a few things from the outer aisles. Almost everything else I buy is frozen, in a colorful box, or in a bag—things I love eating and, with the boys around, will have an excuse to.

When I get home, Bruce is waiting for me on my front porch, where he is most evenings when I get home from work. He doesn't wait for me to let him inside through the front door. As soon as he sees my car, he zooms into the garage, then greets me at my driver's-side door. I give him the rubdown he demands once I'm out and carry all the groceries I bought inside to the kitchen, with him bouncing at my heels.

Wednesday, when I got off work, I bought him the biggest bag of dog treats I could find and put them on the counter in a canister next to Mouse's treats. He now knows they're there, and he also knows I'll give him one as soon as I reach the kitchen. Before I have a chance to give one to him, the doorbell rings. Tyler smiles at me when I open the door, and like always, his presence makes me feel a little off kilter.

"Hey." He leans down and presses a kiss to my cheek, which leaves me stunned. He's never put his lips on me before, and it feels like they're imprinted into my skin.

"I'm just putting away groceries." I turn away from him, not wanting to make a friendly kiss to the cheek awkward. He follows me to the kitchen while holding a bag of Chinese food. When we get there, I go right to Bruce's treat jar and pull out a bacon strip for him. He sits, and I give it to him. I then watch him run off with it in his mouth.

"What is all this?" Tyler asks, looking at the stack of frozen pizzas, gallon of ice cream, box of pancake mix, and assortment of chips, cookies, and candy on the counter.

"I think I told you that Owen and Isaac are coming over tomorrow."

"You did." He picks up a bag of chips. "You weren't joking when you said you're working on being their favorite aunt."

"I'm already their favorite aunt," I state matter-of-factly, glancing at him. "Don't get me wrong—Beth is cool, but she's also a health freak, so they're never thrilled with the idea of hanging with her for a weekend, or even a meal."

"I see." He smiles as he starts to help me put stuff away.

"I should also say that spending time with them gives me an excuse to eat junk food for a couple days without feeling guilty about it."

"Why would you feel guilty about eating junk food?" he asks as I shove the chips into the cupboard.

"When my jeans are so tight that I have to lie down on my bed to button them up, it's not a good feeling. I don't always make the best choices at the grocery store. I try, but colorful things catch my attention and throw me off track."

His eyes slide over me from head to toe, making my skin feel hot. "You're beautiful, babe. You have an amazing body. I don't think you need to worry about having junk food from time to time."

Not sure how to respond, I don't say anything. I go back to putting stuff away, and once we're done, he unpacks the Chinese food. We carry our takeout containers to the living room, where we've eaten dinner the last few nights, and I pass him the remote so he can find something for us to watch. I dig into my sweet-and-sour chicken with fried rice and try not to moan. I love Chinese food—really, I love any kind of takeout. There's nothing better than eating food you didn't have to cook.

"I work tomorrow, but I'll come over for dinner, if you're cool with that," he says when I have a forkful of goodness close to my mouth.

I meet his gaze and smile. "I'm cool with it. The boys already know you, so I'm sure they'll be happy to have you hanging with us."

He nods with a small smile, and we both go back to eating and watching the crime show he ended up on. Once I'm stuffed, I set my dish on the coffee table and lean back against the edge of the couch, tucking my feet under me.

"Are you tired?" he asks after he sets his empty dish next to mine and slouches toward me on the couch.

I shake my head. "Not really. The last few days have been busy, but it hasn't been insane. Most days are filled with my scheduled clients. I haven't had a lot of walk-ins this last week, so I've been steady but not overwhelmed with work," I explain. "How much longer until you guys are done with the church?"

"We should finish Tuesday if things go as planned. When this job is finished, I'll be working Monday through Friday. The hotel doesn't want work done on the weekends, since that's their busiest time of the week."

"I get that." I know I wouldn't want to hear construction if I were on a vacation for a weekend. Actually, I'd probably demand my money back if I had to deal with construction while I was supposed to be on vacation.

He reaches out with his hand, and my eyes drop to it as it lands softly on my knee. "I want to take you out to dinner next Saturday." My heart starts to pound hard against my rib cage, and I lift my eyes to his. "I hope by then I'll have given you plenty of time to get to know me so we can move on from what we are now."

"What?" The word comes out in a hushed tone as I look into his eyes. *Is he saying what I think he's saying?*

"As much as I like just hanging with you, baby, you gotta know it's killing me not to kiss you or touch you like I want to."

Oh my God.

"I—"

"I wanted you to get to know me," he says, cutting me off. "I wanted to be sure before I made a move." His hand moves, and his fingers land gently on my cheek. "The thing is, I like everything about you, and every time you open your mouth, I have to fight to keep from getting hard or kissing you." His expression softens. "I told myself I'd take this slow for you. I've been working on doing that, but I don't know how much longer I'll be able to hold myself in check when it comes to you." His eyes drop to my mouth, and I lick my lips as he does the same.

I hear him groan deep in his chest, and that sound vibrates through me. I don't know who moves first, but our mouths collide, and a frenzy ensues. I touch my tongue to his bottom lip, and he groans again, wrapping his arms around me, pulling me against his big warm body and adjusting me until I'm straddling him. When his tongue slips between my lips, his taste explodes across my taste buds, and I latch on to him, kissing him back and drinking him in.

I can't get enough, and judging by his hands roaming over me and his lips exploring mine, he feels the same. I've never been kissed like he's kissing me. I've never felt every single cell in my body light up and come alive from a kiss. I knew I liked him, but his telling me that he was giving me a chance to get to know him is the sweetest thing anyone has ever said to me before. What I've found out these last few days with him wouldn't have been possible if we'd been doing what we're doing now. Lord knows I wouldn't have even thought about getting to know him, because I would have only been concerned with getting his mouth on mine and his hands on my body.

"I'm glad you placed us in the friend zone." I grind against him, feeling his hard length between us. As happy as I am about that, I'm happier that I get to feel his lips and touch, that I get to experience all of him now.

"We were never in the friend zone, baby." He drags my top off over my head and then pulls down the cups of my lace bra until my breasts are exposed. He drinks me in, and his eyes grow darker. "My thoughts about you were never friendly." He captures one nipple between his lips, sucking hard and causing my back to arch and my head to fall back toward my shoulders. When he moves to my neglected nipple, I cry out, clutching his shoulders while rolling my hips into his. He releases my nipple and cups both my breasts in his big hands, and his thumbs skim over the tightened buds.

I focus on his face, and when our eyes lock, I whisper, "Please take me to bed." At this point, I'm not above begging him for what I need.

Without a word, he lifts us both off the couch with his hands under my ass. A thrill of desire and excitement courses through me, and I lock my legs around his hips. Our mouths meet again as he carries me down the hallway toward my bedroom, this kiss slower than the previous ones on the couch. My back lowers to the bed, and he comes down on top of me with his heavy weight.

I move, adjusting my arms so I can slide my hands up the back of his shirt. I'm greeted with warm skin that's soft compared to the muscles underneath. He pulls his mouth from mine and leans back, looking into my eyes once more as he slips his hands behind my back and unhooks my bra, while I pull up his shirt until he's forced to lean back to remove it. I take in every detail of him—his wide, hard chest, defined abs, and the small trail of hair that disappears into the waistband of his jeans.

My hands shake as I place them against his skin and slide them down over the contoured muscles.

He pops the button on my jeans, then releases the zipper, and his fingers slide across my stomach just under the edge of my panties. My muscles contract, and more wet heat pools between my legs. I lift my hips as he pulls my jeans and panties off, tossing them out of the way. Completely naked and exposed, I don't feel vulnerable or nervous. My body is on fire, and my mind is foggy with need.

When his hands slide up to my knees, I open for him. His head drops forward while his light touch moves up my inner thighs. I don't have a moment to prepare for his mouth on me, his hot, wet tongue sliding up before his lips close around my clit. My eyes roll back into my head, and my fingers lace into his hair, holding him exactly where he is. My feet dig into the mattress, and he groans as I grind myself against him while he flicks my clit and sucks it hard.

As he slips two fingers inside me, rubbing them against my G-spot, my head thrashes, and stars begin dancing behind my closed eyelids as I come. Still on the high from my orgasm, I feel his lips trail to my knee, and I slowly open my eyes. I watch him with my chest heaving as he gets off the bed to remove his boots and take off his jeans and boxers.

He takes out a foil packet from his wallet, then tosses the wallet to my bedside table, where it slides across the smooth surface before landing on the floor. When my gaze meets his, I watch his eyes roam over me as he wraps his hand around his hard length. My mouth waters. He's perfect everywhere; even his cock is perfect, long and thick, the veins defined as they stand out.

"You're beautiful," I breathe.

"I was thinking the same thing." He places one knee on the bed and then the other, settling between my legs. His palms wrap around my face, and his fingers slowly slide back into my hair. "The first time I saw you, you took my breath away. I thought I dreamed you up. There was no other explanation for the most beautiful woman I've ever seen just falling through my window." He grins, and I start to laugh. "I love that sound."

My heart skips a beat on the word *love*, and I lean up, pressing my lips to his, not wanting him to see what he already means to me in such a short time.

He takes over the kiss, and we explore each other, using our hands, lips, teeth, and tongues. When I wrap my hand around his hard length, I listen to him hiss. "Fuck."

"I need you," I whisper against his lips.

"You've got me." He thrusts into my hold. "Fuck, you've had me since the moment we met." He leans back on his knees and rips open the condom packet with his teeth. He slides it down his length, and my pussy contracts in anticipation of having him inside me.

When he leans over me, his weight settling between my thighs and his fist by my head, I lift my hips. I feel the head of his cock where I need him most and moan. I can't wait to feel him filling me. I can't wait to feel all of him. He slides inside me slowly, breathing heavily, and when the tip of his cock hits my G-spot, I circle him with my legs. His body stills for a moment as I adjust to his size. He begins to move, his pace speeding up, and I urge him on, needing more.

"You're going to kill me." His breath whispers across my lips as his pace picks up.

I lift my hips to meet his thrusts and circle my hips. God, it's never been this good. I have never felt anything like this before. I hold on to him with my arms and legs, accepting all of him, everything he wants to give me. I know I'm close again, and I know exactly what I need to get me there. I start to lower my hand between us, but he stops me, taking both my hands and pulling them up over my head. He kisses me again and leans down, pulling one nipple and then the other into his mouth. He grinds his hips into mine, his pubic bone rubbing my clit. I start to spasm around him, and he lets go of one of my hands, then moves his hand between us, rolling his thumb against my clit as he leans back and pounds into me with hard thrusts.

I cry out, "Tyler!" as my body arches off the bed. His cock hits my G-spot as his thumb rolls my clit. I come, and he comes with me, his thrusts turning erratic until he stills deep inside me, his weight pressing me into the bed. He buries his face against my neck, and I encircle him with all four of my limbs, holding him as tightly as I can.

His lips touch my neck, and he leans back, looking into my eyes. "You okay?"

"Yes." I lift one hand to his jaw. He slowly pulls out, and I mewl from the sudden loss, and then I roll to my side and grab on to him when he starts to get off the bed.

Pausing, he looks at me over his shoulder, then turns to face me completely, with his gaze roaming my face and body. For the first time with him, I feel exposed and weak. Leaning down, he places his face close to mine and slides his palm up my hip, speaking quietly. "I'm not leaving. I just need to take care of this condom and get something to clean you up."

"Oh . . . of course." I lick my lips.

His expression softens, and he brushes his mouth against mine, then my bare shoulder. "Be right back."

I nod and watch him walk naked to my bathroom and flip on the light. I roll to my back and look at the ceiling, pulling in a breath and wondering if this whole thing is too good to be true. When he comes back a few minutes later, he uses a washcloth to clean me up—something no one has ever done before. After he takes the cloth back to the bathroom, he comes back and gets into bed with me, pulling me against his warm chest.

"What time are your nephews getting here tomorrow?"

"Probably around ten." I tip my head back to look at him.

"I gotta be at the jobsite by seven."

"Okay," I say as he rolls toward me.

"I'm sorry."

"For what?" Unease suddenly curls in my belly.

"You're gonna be tired tomorrow."

"What?"

He doesn't respond with words. He kisses me again and then does other things to me, which means neither of us falls asleep until the sun is already brightening the sky.

"I don't think I understand this game at all," I mumble as I watch Owen playing *Fortnite*. Isaac giggles from my side, where he's digging into a bag of Cheetos and smiling, his adorable mouth covered in orange dust. It's been three hours of them playing this game, and although I consider myself up to date on most things, I don't get the appeal of this at all. "I think we need a change of venue," I announce while I get off the couch. "You." I point at Isaac. "Wash your face. And you." I look at Owen. "Turn off the game."

"But—" Owen starts, glancing between the TV and me.

I cut him off before he can start complaining. "We're going to Dave & Buster's. I have the urge to kick both your butts and finally redeem myself as the all-time champion of *Jurassic Park* and *Zombie Apocalypse*."

"Right on!" Isaac jumps up off the couch, sending the bag of Cheetos on his lap to the floor, and he starts to clean up the mess.

"Heck yeah!" Owen gets up and shuts off the game without saving what he's accomplished in the last few hours. "We're so gonna kick your butt," he announces with a smug smile.

"We'll see, kid, but I wouldn't get your hopes up. Clean up so we can go."

I leave the living room and grab my phone from the kitchen. Tyler said he'd be here for dinner, so I want to let him know dinner will now be at Dave & Buster's. Video games, burgers, fries, and fun is my idea of the perfect night.

Me: Change of plans. Heading to Dave & Busters with the boys.

Not even a minute after I send the text, he replies.

Tyler: See you there, baby.

I smile at my phone. I get dressed, since I'm in my lounge clothes, then get on my shoes and coat before grabbing my purse and ushering the two boys into my car.

"Kill them all!" I shout at the screen as Isaac and I attempt for the fifth time in a row to beat the level we're on in *Zombie Apocalypse.*

"Shoot him, shoot him!" he yells back as a zombie stumbles toward me. I don't get in a kill shot, and my side of the screen goes red as the zombie takes me out.

"My turn." Owen slides his card through the reader, and I get out of the small enclosed booth and hand him my gun. He and his brother start shouting at each other, and I shout along with them and cheer them on. When a hand wraps around my stomach, I jump and look behind me.

"Hey, baby." Tyler. Tyler—looking as handsome as ever, wearing a backward baseball cap and a smile. "It took me forever to find you in this chaos." His lips brush over mine. "Tried to call, but you didn't pick up."

"We're killing zombies."

"I see that," he says, smiling at the boys, who are still yelling at the game. "Have you guys eaten yet?" He looks down at me.

"We've been waiting on you." I turn around to face him. "How was work?"

"Work." He presses his lips to my forehead, and I smile.

"After this game, we'll find a table."

"Before I get a chance to kick your ass? I think not, baby." He pulls out a card from his pocket, holding it between two fingers, and I swear I feel myself fall in love with him in that instant. I haven't met a guy before who's cool with hanging out at an arcade and acting like a kid.

"As if you could." I smile up at him, and his eyes roam my face before they drop to my smiling lips.

"So gonna take you out." He kisses me. It's not soft; it's wet and deep and filled with a million different things that make me hope I'm not wrong about him.

When he pulls his mouth from mine, I'm breathing heavily, but I still have it in me to be sassy. "You are not kicking my butt. I'm the champion."

"We'll see." He grins at me before he wraps his arm around my shoulders and leans into the enclosed booth where Isaac and Owen are. "When you two are done, I'm going to show your aunt how to be a gracious loser."

Both boys glance at him with smiles; then they both start to shout about me getting my butt kicked by Tyler as they're killed off in the game.

"Slide your card!" I shout at Isaac a while later as I pull back on the trigger of the plastic gun.

"It doesn't have any more money!" he shouts back frantically as he taps the machine, trying to get it to work.

"Crap." My head falls forward in defeat. I'm dead, beaten by Tyler, who's now moving on to the next level in the game.

"I'm hungry," Owen says, and Tyler instantly lowers his gun, even though he's still kicking butt, and looks at my nephews.

"Let's get a table, then." He places his controller back in the holder, and we both scoot out of the booth. When we reach the front of the restaurant, they tell us the wait is about thirty minutes, but they give us a buzzer to let us know when our table will be ready. To kill time, Tyler and the boys play basketball while I dump money into the claw machine in an attempt to win a stuffed unicorn I know Mia would love, even though there's a cute panda I want for myself.

Almost twenty dollars later, while I'm cursing the stupid machine, Tyler comes over with Owen and Isaac, and he takes over. On his first try, he wins a panda bear, and on his second, he wins the unicorn. I'm not gracious in accepting his winnings, and he laughs along with both boys as I complain about the machine taking all my money.

When our table is ready and we're seated, the boys crowd into one side while Tyler and I take the other. We all order hamburgers and fries, and when we're finished with our meals, we get three different types of dessert to share. After we're stuffed, we play a few more games before Tyler helps me load the two tired boys back into my car. I take them back to my house, get them ready for bed, and tuck them in for the night, loving the smiles both of them have on their faces.

It was a good night—one of the best I've ever had—and I know that's because I spent it not only with my nephews whom I adore but also with Tyler, a guy who was totally cool with eating hamburgers and fries for dinner and playing games with two loud kids, and he had a good time doing it.

Suggestion 7

LEAVE ALL THE GOOD STUFF OUT

LEAH

"Thanks for looking after the boys," my brother says as he gives me a hug, and I lean back just enough so I can see his face.

"You know they're always welcome to come stay with me," I reply as he lets me go when Angie comes over to us, and he wraps his arm around her shoulders. "Did you guys have fun?" I look between them. They look relaxed and rested, the opposite of how they looked when they dropped the boys off Saturday morning. I get it now—having two wild boys around to entertain is tiring, and for them, that's their life every day; they rarely get a break.

"We had a really great time." He kisses the top of Angie's head, and her cheeks get pink.

"I see." I grin knowingly at the two of them.

Angie rolls her eyes at me before she looks around the living room and asks, "Did they happen to eat any veggies while we were gone?"

I look at the coffee table, which is still covered with pizza plates, half-eaten bags of chips, and candy wrappers.

"Are potatoes considered a veggie?" I ask her, and she laughs. "What about the little peppers on pizza?" She shakes her head, smiling, and I shrug, not feeling even a little bad.

"Well, I'm going to make sure they get all their stuff," she says before turning toward the hall that leads to my spare bedroom, where the boys are packing up their things.

"I see Tyler's here," Noah says quietly while studying me. He is here, but he got a phone call about two seconds after I answered the door for my brother, and he went to the kitchen to take the call. He's been here all morning. He came over before the boys were awake, so he and I made out in my bed until the boys got up. He made all of us french toast for breakfast, which the boys loved just as much as I do. And after we ate, we went to the aquarium and spent a few hours there before coming back to my house so the boys could play their game and we could have a late lunch of frozen pizzas.

"He is here, but why are we whispering about it?" I whisper back.

"I don't know. Are you two still just friends?" he asks, and I shrug. He snorts. "That didn't last long."

"Whatever."

"I like him. He's the first guy you've dated that I actually like."

"You liked Chris," I remind him.

"I tolerated Chris because you liked him so much," he says softly, and I feel my brows pull together over my eyes.

"Really? I always thought you liked him."

"No, and neither did Dad or Ben."

"None of you ever said anything to me." I frown at him.

"Why would we? We know how you are. You're stubborn and have always had to figure things out for yourself. Telling you we didn't like Chris for you wouldn't have changed anything. All it would've done was just create tension."

"Maybe you're right," I mutter. The truth is I've always had to learn by fire.

"I'm just letting you know that we approve of Tyler."

"You've had one meal with him," I say, and something seeps into his expression that I've never seen before.

"I watched him with you, watched the way he looked at you and the way he looked after you. I also saw him win over Dad—who's easy to get along with but not easy to win over. He's cool. I like him."

"I like him too. A lot," I whisper. It's becoming more and more clear that Tyler is just who he appears to be, and I really do like him.

"If things work out, I'll be happy for you. If they don't, I might still keep him as a friend." He grins and I laugh.

"Whatever. You should probably go help your wife pack up your sons so she doesn't lose her glow."

"You're probably right." He kisses the top of my head before disappearing down the hall.

I start to gather all the food off the coffee table, and I carry it into the kitchen. When Tyler sees me step through the doorway, he smiles, and my heart flips. Yes, I really like him. I drop the stuff in my hands on the counter, then go back to the living room to get the rest. When I reach the kitchen again, he's putting stuff away while still talking on the phone. I dump the leftover pizza crusts in the garbage and rinse off the plates. I start to place them in the dishwasher just as he hangs up on his call.

"Everything okay?" I glance in his direction before I close the door on the dishwasher.

"Yeah, that was Scott. He's the friend I told you about, the one who offered me the job." I nod, remembering him telling me about him. "He wanted to make sure we're still on track to finish the church this week."

"He doesn't come to check on things while you're working?"

"No." He smiles. "He trusts me to get the job done. He flips houses—that's his main gig. This business was a side gig. He didn't expect it to take off like it did, but with the boom in the economy, he had jobs lining up. That's why he called me. He didn't want to turn down money, and he knew I wasn't happy where I was."

"Why weren't you happy?" I lean against the counter, and he gets close to me, placing his hand on my hip.

"I worked construction in Tennessee. I did it for years. My boss had promised me that he was going to move me up to foreman, but it never happened. I was in charge, but I wasn't making the money I should've been making for the time I was putting in or the work I was doing."

"That sucks."

"It worked out in the end," he says, using his hand on my hip to pull me against him. "I'm not going to complain about the way things turned out."

My belly dips, and I start to lean up to kiss him but stop when I hear "Aunt Leah!" shouted by two different voices.

I step around Tyler and stumble backward as Isaac runs into me, wrapping his arms around my waist. "Thank you. We had so much fun! Can we come back soon?"

I slide my fingers into his hair and smile into his happy face. "Yes, anytime you want."

"Yes!" he shouts, jumping away from me and throwing his arms in the air.

"Thank you, Aunt Leah," Owen says, coming toward me. I hold my arms open, and he rolls his eyes before he wraps his arms around my waist. "It was fun."

"Duh, dude. Who's the coolest aunt in the world?"

"You are." He rolls his eyes again, like *You're a dork*, and I smile before leaning down to kiss his forehead and then his cheeks just to annoy him. When I finally let him go, he goes to his dad, who wraps a hand around his shoulder.

"Thanks, sis." Noah looks at me, then addresses Tyler. "Will we see you next Sunday?"

"Yeah," Tyler answers, sliding his hand around my waist, and I catch Angie's wide-eyed look, but I don't acknowledge it even with a look of my own.

"See you both then," Noah says, and he looks down at his boys. "Who wants Steak 'n Shake for dinner?" Both boys yell in happiness before saying goodbye and rushing to get out of the house.

"I don't know how either of them are hungry," I say, looking at Angie.

"They are bottomless pits. I don't know where they put the food they consume on a daily basis. All I know is that my grocery bill would give most people heart palpitations."

"That I believe." I laugh as she comes over to give me a hug.

"Seriously, thank you for this weekend," she whispers with her arms around me.

"Anytime." I hug her back, and then I watch my brother take his wife's hand and lead her out of the house with the boys running ahead of them to their SUV. I wave at them, standing on my porch as they back out of my driveway, and then sigh as Tyler places his arm around my shoulders.

"It's going to be so quiet with them gone."

"Yeah," he agrees, turning me back toward the house. When we get inside, I head for the kitchen. I'm not really hungry right now, but I know I will be in a few hours. I'm searching for something to make for dinner when I feel Tyler get close to my back. "What are you doing?"

"Looking for something to make for dinner."

"Are you hungry?" he asks, and I feel his lips touch my neck.

"Not right now." I open the freezer and move stuff around to see what I have.

"I *am* hungry." He nips my neck, and my whole body tingles.

"You are?"

"Yeah." His nose trails up until his lips rest against the shell of my ear. "I think you should feed me."

74

I don't have a chance to ask him what he's hungry for. He spins me around to face him; then his mouth lands on mine. He picks me up and carries me to my bedroom, where he does, in fact, have something to eat. And I have to say I probably enjoy it more than he does, but then again, when we leave my room much later, both of us are completely satisfied but absolutely starving.

An odd quacking noise pulls me from sleep, and I blink my eyes open and lift my head off Tyler's chest as he shifts in bed, still holding me against him. "What's that horrible noise?" I cover my ear that's not pressed to his chest.

"My alarm clock," he tells me as the sound is cut off. He slides his hand down my back to my bottom and squeezes one of my ass cheeks. "I gotta get up."

"Why does your alarm sound like a dying duck?"

He laughs and kisses the top of my head. "It's the only sound I knew would get me out of your bed."

My body melts deeper into him, and I look at the closed window behind me and notice it's still dark outside. It's fall, but it's never dark when I get up in the morning. "What time is it?" I don't have an alarm clock. I always just use my cell phone, but it's out of reach, so I can't grab it to look at the screen and check the time.

"Four," he says before I feel his lips touch the top of my head.

"You actually have to get up at four in the morning to go to work?"

"Unfortunately." He rolls me to my back and places his face close enough to mine that I'm able to make out a few of his features in the dark. "I need to finish this job by deadline, which means I need to be at the jobsite early."

"I'm sorry."

"Not as sorry as I am." The hold he still has on my bottom tightens, and I feel his erection press into my thigh. He touches his mouth to my smiling lips, then groans. "Fuck, I can't wait until this job is done." *Me neither*, I agree silently as he pulls away and gets off the bed. "Gonna shower here, then take Bruce home."

"He's okay. I can take him to your place later," I tell him as I drag his pillow to my chest and wrap my arms around it.

"You sure?"

"Of course."

"Thanks, baby." He leans over me and kisses me again; then I watch his shadowy form head for the bathroom. He waits until he's inside and the door is closed to turn on the light, and then I listen to my shower start. My eyes get too heavy to keep open, and I fall asleep while he showers but wake up for a couple of seconds when he kisses me once more and tells me that he's going to leave his key for me on the counter.

I mumble, "Have a good day," then fall back asleep before he even pulls his fist out of the bed.

I wake up at eight when my alarm goes off, feeling like I haven't slept at all, and stumble out of bed and into the shower. By the time I'm dressed and ready for work, it's a little after nine. I feed Mouse before I take Bruce home and feed him. When I get to work, it's already ten and just about thirty minutes before my first client is due to arrive. Grams, who is with a client, tells me that my mom is out getting coffee but will be back soon. Knowing today will be busy, I get things ready at my station and make sure I have the supplies I need before I do a quick sweep of the floor.

When my mom gets back, she gives me a kiss to my cheek and hands me a cup of coffee that I'm more than a little thankful for. I don't know why, but today I feel like I just can't wake up. When Deloris arrives right on time, I take her to the back of the salon. I add a blue toner to the shampoo, which will take out the yellow in her gray hair, and let it set for about ten minutes while she talks about her kids, who are not actually kids but adults in their fifties. Like always, I nod as she complains about them.

Deloris has lived in town for ages. She used to own the florist shop down the street but gave the business up to her kids when her arthritis got so bad she was no longer able to make the floral arrangements. Even though she no longer owns the business, she still considers it hers and is never happy with the way her kids are running things. Having gotten flowers from their shop on my birthday from my parents, I think they're doing a great job, but what do I know?

Once her hair is washed and conditioned, I lead her back to my chair and give her a trim before I start the process of drying her hair and curling it at the same time with a small roller brush.

When I hear the bell over the door ding, I turn my head and start to smile at whoever is coming into the shop. I see it's Charles, and I bite back a curse. He messaged me a few days after our date to see when I'd be available to go out with him again. I didn't want to be rude, so I told him that I was slammed with work but would let him know. I haven't messaged him back since then and assumed he'd take the hint. Apparently, he didn't.

"Hey, Charles," I say over the noise of the blow-dryer I'm still using.

"Leah." He smiles at me, then looks around, smiling at the women who are waiting or already getting their hair done. I swear I hear a few of the women sigh as he comes toward me in his custom suit, with his hair perfectly styled and his tan probably purchased from the same place Grams gets hers done down the block.

I turn to face him when he reaches my station, and I flip off the dryer. "How's it going?"

"Good." He leans down, kissing my cheek, and I fight the urge to wipe the feel of his lips away. "I was in the area and thought we could get lunch."

"I'm sorry." I gesture with the round brush in my hand to Deloris's head. "I'm working."

"We're almost done, aren't we?" I look at Deloris in the mirror and see she has a hopeful light in her eyes and a helpful smile on her wrinkled face.

Crap.

"You're just about done," I agree with her, then look at Charles. "I really am sorry, but I have a few more appointments after I finish with Deloris."

"I don't mind waiting while you get something to eat," my next client, Sandy, announces from one of the three chairs at the front under the window that looks out to the street. My eyes meet her big brown ones, and she smiles wide, showing off her too-white-to-be-real teeth.

Sandy is a beauty pageant coach. She always has on a full face of makeup and hair so big it's a surprise she can fit through most doors. She comes in once a week for a wash and set and for me to use a can of hair spray on her head. She's sweet to her core and such a romantic that she always has a romance novel in her hand. I adore her, but right now I want to strangle her.

"Thanks, Sandy. That's sweet of you to offer, but if I push your appointment back, my day will be derailed," I explain gently.

"Bummer." Her face falls.

"Sorry," I say, looking at Charles once more.

"Another time."

I don't nod or agree. I'll call him later and let him know I'm seeing someone. I hope I can save us both the embarrassment by not doing it right now. "I hope you have a good day."

"You too, sweetheart." He kisses my cheek again just as the bell dings once more. When I glance over to see who has come in, my stomach bottoms out.

This cannot be happening.

Tyler's eyes lock on mine, and I swear it takes every bit of strength I have not to run screaming from the salon. "Babe," he says to me, and then he moves his eyes to Charles, who's still standing right next to me. "What's up?"

Charles puffs out his chest. "You're her neighbor? The one with the dog."

"Tyler." He holds out his hand.

"Charles," he says, wrapping his hand tightly around Tyler's, and then I watch him wince before he pulls his hand back and flexes it at his side before he focuses on me. "Hopefully, I'll see you soon."

God, this is so awkward. I should have just told him that I wasn't interested after he messaged me the first time instead of trying to save his feelings. "I—"

"Sorry, bud, but that isn't gonna happen," Tyler announces before I can even get two words out.

"And why exactly is that?" Charles asks, sounding pompous as he lifts his hands to the lapels of his suit, grasping them while eyeing Tyler.

"Tyler and I are seeing each other," I admit quietly. I don't want Tyler to think I'm trying to hide him, and I know that's exactly what he will assume if I'm not honest right now. I feel every eye in the place is on the three of us, and I have no doubt that the women taking in this scene are going to spread far and wide what they saw at the salon this afternoon.

Charles looks down at me. "You didn't mention that when we were at dinner."

"We weren't seeing each other when you and I went on our date," I reply, hating how awkward this situation is. "But now we are." I really wish the ground would just open up and swallow me whole already. I feel my face getting hotter from the attention surrounding us.

"I see." He lifts his chin, his jaw now hard. "In that case, I'll just be going."

"Sorry," I say to his back as he leaves the salon, swinging the door open with more force than is necessary.

"You didn't need to turn that into a pissing contest," I tell Tyler, and I know I hear my mom laugh from her station a few feet away.

"I wasn't the one who tried to prove his manhood with a handshake," Tyler states. Then he asks softly, "Why was he here?" Even though his voice is low, I still hear annoyance in his tone.

"He wanted to take her to lunch," Deloris says helpfully. "I see now why she didn't agree to go with him. I don't think I would have, either, if I were her."

Lord, save me.

"Why didn't you just say you were already seeing someone?" Sandy asks loudly from across the salon.

"She obviously didn't want to embarrass him," Deloris snaps. "You know how men get." She waves her hand around. "They're sensitive about being turned down, especially by a beautiful woman."

"Too true," Grams mumbles, and I know she's smiling, even though I'm not looking at her to see it.

"Did you need something?" I ask Tyler. He's never come here before; really, I didn't think he knew where the shop was. Then again, there is only one Bleach Bomb Shell's in town.

"I was in the area and had some time. I thought I'd swing by and see if you could get away for a break to grab something to eat."

"I really wish I could." I want to take Sandy up on her earlier offer, but it wouldn't feel right if I did it now.

"That's all right. I'll see you for dinner in a few hours. I'm cooking at my place."

"All right," I agree, and he leans down, touching his mouth to mine and surprising me.

"Have a good day, baby." His eyes scan my face; then his fingers graze my cheek.

"You too." I watch him kiss my mom's cheek and then my grams's before he goes to the door. He gives me one last look before he pulls the door open and disappears.

I glance around and note everyone is now looking at me.

"I'm going to go out on a limb and guess that you and Tyler are a little more than friends now," Mom says, and I bite my lip. I haven't told her or Grams about the change in our relationship. I guess now I don't need to. The whole kiss on the lips and cheek touch are more difficult to explain than the hand-holding.

"Um . . ."

"Spill while you finish my hair," Deloris demands. "And don't leave any of the good stuff out."

"Yeah, sugar, don't leave any of the good stuff out," Grams agrees, giving me a wink.

I sigh, start up my blow-dryer, and then spill about Tyler and me. Unfortunately for all the women listening, I leave all the good stuff out, because that's for me and me alone.

"Tell me what happened with Charles," Tyler says as he lifts me up to sit on the counter next to the stove, where he's been cooking. I thought maybe we would skip over this conversation since he didn't mention it when I got to his house, and I've been here for over an hour now.

When I got home from work, Bruce was at my house to greet me like he normally is, and Tyler came to walk me over after I sent him a text and told him I would be at his place after changing my clothes and feeding Mouse. When we got here, he started dinner, and we both chatted about work while I played with Bruce, until Bruce decided he wanted to head outside. I thought for sure Tyler was letting go of what had happened this afternoon.

No such luck. When he looks at me, raising a brow, I sigh and tell him, "After our date, he texted, asking when we could have dinner again. I told him I was busy with work but I'd let him know. I never messaged him again, so he stopped by the shop today."

"So he didn't take the hint when you never messaged him back?" Tyler questions while I take a sip of wine and watch him stir a jar of pasta sauce into the sausage, eggplant, pepper, garlic, and onion mixture he's already cooked.

I shrug. "It's my fault. I really should have just told him then that I wasn't interested. I just felt bad. I didn't want to hurt his feelings."

"He could have just taken the hint," he says while looking over at me. "He knew you weren't interested when you didn't call him. Him showing up at the salon was about him putting you on the spot and forcing you to go to lunch. That old lady was right—his ego was bruised, and he knew if he cornered you at work, you likely wouldn't refuse him."

"Maybe." I take another sip of wine.

"Known guys like him my whole life, baby. He's not stupid. He had a plan showing up at your job, especially knowing that your mom likes him."

"So are you still on track with the church?" I don't want to talk about Charles—not now, not ever.

He grins at me, then asks, "Trying to change the subject?"

I roll my eyes. "Yes. Is it working?"

He sets down the wooden spoon in his hand and comes over to me, pushing my knees apart and settling his hips between my thighs. "I don't like that guy in your space."

"He's not a threat," I say as I stare into his eyes, swearing I see jealousy there.

Why do I like that idea so much? I've never made a man jealous before. If I'm honest, it makes me feel strangely secure in the way he feels about me.

"You're right—he's not, but I still don't like him putting you on the spot. Hopefully, he doesn't do it again. If he does, he and I are gonna have a chat." I notice his jaw is hard before he brushes his lips over mine. He leans back, and his fingers curve around my neck. "Now, I wanted to talk to you about something."

Oh no. Now what?

"Okay," I agree, sounding reluctant, and he smiles before quickly brushing his mouth over mine again and pulling away.

"Thanksgiving."

"Thanksgiving?" My head tips to the side in question.

"I'm gonna drive home to spend the holiday with my folks." My heart sinks. Thanksgiving is still a few weeks away, but it won't be long till it's here, and then he'll be leaving. Even if it's for just a few days, I don't like the way that makes my insides feel. "I was hoping you'd be able to get away for the weekend and go with me."

"To spend Thanksgiving with your family?" Why does my voice sound funny and my chest feel so warm all of a sudden?

"Yeah."

"Do you . . . do you think that's a good idea?"

His brows pull together. "Why the hell wouldn't it be a good idea?"

Because meeting your family is a huge step, I obviously don't say. "I don't know. It's—"

He cuts me off. "I had dinner with your family, and I'll be at dinner with you this Sunday." Then his voice gets softer. "I'm hoping you like what we're building as much as I do. I know we're just getting to know each other, but I know what I feel when I'm with you, and I know I want more of that. I really fucking hope you feel the same."

Holy moly.

I already feel the same, but hearing him say he wants more—no game playing, no doubt or worrying—I know I'd be an idiot if I didn't take him up on his offer to spend Thanksgiving with him and his parents, no matter how much the idea freaks me out.

"I think I can probably swing Thanksgiving," I murmur.

"Good," he grunts, giving me a swift kiss before letting me go and stepping back. He picks up the wooden spoon once more and then asks, "Are you hungry?"

"Yeah," I answer, even though the last thing on my mind right now is food.

"I'll serve us up, baby. Let Bruce back in."

"Sure." I set my wineglass aside and hop down off the counter. I walk through the kitchen, then the living room, and open the front door. I expect Bruce to be sitting there waiting, so when he's not, I call out to him. When he doesn't appear after I've called for him three times in a row, panic starts to fill me. I step out onto the porch and shout his name. Since I've been around, he's never once wandered more than the distance between Tyler's house and mine. I run down the stairs, yelling his name while heading for my house. When I reach my front porch, arms wrap around me from behind.

"He's not here," I cry as I search the dark for him. "Where is he?"

"We'll find him. He never goes far," Tyler assures me, leading me across the lawn and back to his house.

"He always comes when you or I call him," I point out, scanning the dark street again when we reach his porch.

"He'll be okay. He probably smelled something and took off after it. He'll be back."

Even though I hear the assurance in his voice, I don't agree. My insides are a mess, and I know something is wrong; this isn't like him. We get inside, and he places me on the couch before heading back out. I listen to him shout Bruce's name, and more worry fills the pit of my stomach. When he comes back, I get up.

"Has he ever done this before? Taken off and not come back when he's called?" I question.

"No." He rips his fingers through his hair.

I get closer to him, resting my hands against his chest. "I'll get my car, and you take your truck. We'll split up and search the area. Maybe he wandered too far and doesn't know the way back home."

He looks doubtful, but still he leans down, resting his forehead against mine. "All right—get your car, and make sure you've got your phone on you."

"We'll find him," I whisper.

"We will." He presses his lips hard against mine, then lets me go. I watch him as he goes to the kitchen and turns off the stove. I move to the door when he's done before running to my house and letting myself inside. I grab my car key and purse, then go get in my car and back out, and I see Tyler getting into his truck. I give him a wave while rolling down my window, and I start shouting for Bruce, driving slowly down each block, scanning the yards and the street.

Thirty minutes into looking, Tyler calls, so I answer using my hands-free system.

"Did you find him?"

"No, but I got stopped by one of our neighbors. They said they thought they saw him being loaded up by animal control."

"What?" I breathe, gripping the steering wheel tightly.

"It's dark, so he wasn't sure. He felt like shit he didn't come over after he saw what he saw. Apparently, Bruce is well liked on the block, and when he's out and about, he visits the neighbors and the kids."

"Of course he's well liked. He's a good dog."

"I tried calling animal control. They aren't answering, and the message says they won't be open until the morning."

"Wouldn't they check his collar?" I ask. I pull over to the side of the road and put my car in park.

"No clue, baby, but with Bruce not coming back, I'm thinking it's because he got picked up and doesn't have a choice in the matter."

"I want to keep looking," I say as I pull back onto the road. "Maybe he's still out. Maybe—"

He cuts me off. "Baby, I appreciate that you want to keep searching, but I want you back at my place. If he is out, he'll show up, and if he doesn't, I'll call animal control in the morning as soon as they open."

"What if he's hurt?" My stomach turns at the idea of him being hurt and alone.

"I can't think of that right now, and I don't want you thinking about that either. He'll be okay, and he'll be back. How far are you?"

"I don't know, probably five minutes."

"I'll see you in five then. I'll meet you at your place. You can pack a bag and get Mouse. We'll stay at my house tonight."

"I'll see you there," I agree, but I don't go right home. I drive down a few more blocks, continuing to yell out the window for Bruce while tears fill my eyes. When Tyler calls again, I ignore his call but head back to my house and pull into the garage. Before I can even open the door, Tyler does, and then I'm in his arms.

"Baby, he'll be okay," he says against my ear while rocking me from side to side. "He'll be home tomorrow."

I pull in a few deep breaths and get myself under control. Once my tears have dried up, I let him lead me into my house. He goes in search of Mouse while I pack a bag, and when I'm done, we go to his house. He makes me eat and then takes me to bed, where I spend most of the night wide awake, just in case Bruce comes back.

Suggestion 8

PUT THE PAST IN ITS PLACE

LEAH

As soon as Tyler pulls into a parking spot outside the local Humane Society, I open my door and hop out. I hear him curse but ignore him and run to the front door. This morning he called and asked about Bruce, describing him to the person on the phone as I sat across from him on the bed, biting my nails. Relief filled his eyes, and I knew they had him. My body went slack, the tension I'd held on to all night releasing instantly. I hurried and got dressed, and Tyler did the same; then we drove over here.

Now I want to see my boy. He's not my dog, but I've fallen in love with him, and I don't know what I would do without him.

An arm circles my waist as soon as I wrap my fingers around the handle; then the door is tugged from my grasp as Tyler spins me around. His face lowers toward mine so all I can see are his eyes, and he looks angry. "You ever jump out of my truck before I've put it in park, baby, and you and I are going to have a conversation about spankings."

"W-what?" I stutter, searching his gaze.

"Don't do it again. I know you wanna see Bruce, but I'd like to keep seeing you, so help me out with that," he growls, and I nod, wondering why I am all of a sudden turned on.

I shouldn't be, should I? I've never been spanked in my life. My parents didn't even spank me when I was little. The idea of him doing it should not cause my nipples to tighten and my clit to pulse, but it does.

I lick my lips and then say quietly, "Okay, I'll help you out and not jump out of your truck again."

His eyes search mine, and then his expression shifts, growing dark in the blink of an eye. "Fuck, now I wanna make out with you but can't because we need to get Bruce, and then I need to get to work."

"Then maybe you should let me go so we can do that," I suggest softly while dropping my eyes to his mouth.

He makes a frustrated noise before letting me go. He opens the door without another word and ushers me inside with his hand on my lower back. When we get to the front counter, we ask for Bruce, and they tell us they'll bring him out. I wait with my hand held in Tyler's, bouncing on the balls of my feet. As soon as Bruce comes through a door at the side of the desk, he pulls against the leash around his neck and drags the guy behind him toward us.

"You scared us so badly." I get down on my knees and wrap my arms around his big furry neck as he licks my face and wiggles in happiness against me. "I'm so glad you're okay." I stand back up, and Tyler takes over, giving him attention, and then he orders him to sit, and he does.

"If you guys didn't come to pick him up, I was going to take him home with me," the guy announces, still holding the leash attached to Bruce. "He's a great fricking dog. You really need to make sure he's got a collar and a tag."

At his statement, I glance down and see his collar is missing. "He has a collar. Or he had one."

"I'm the one who picked him up after we got a call about him. He didn't have a collar on when I got him. If he did, I would've called the number on the collar."

"Where did you pick him up?" Tyler questions, and the guy rattles off our street name and then describes my house. "You said someone called about him?"

"Yeah, they said there was a dog that seemed unstable, and they were worried he might hurt someone. When I got there, I found him and brought him back here."

"We'll make sure to keep a better eye on him from now on," Tyler says through clenched teeth. "He's also chipped. Did that come up in the system when you scanned him?"

"Don't have a reader in my truck, and I was going to do a scan this morning when I came in. You called before I got to that."

"Thank you." I grab Tyler's hand and give it a squeeze. "We really appreciate you taking care of him last night."

"No problem, and like I said, he's a great dog—friendly and well trained."

"Do you need anything from us before we go?"

"Nope, you're good. Just get him a collar and make sure he's always got it on. You can keep that leash." He hands it over to me. "We've got a stockpile of them."

"Thanks." I tug on Tyler's hand and get him to follow me outside, and when we reach his truck, he takes it from me. He helps me in before slamming my door and opening the back door for Bruce to hop in. When he's behind the wheel and backing out, I ask, "Are you okay?"

"Not real happy about one of our neighbors calling animal control on my dog, especially when they all know he belongs to me. Everyone around us has spent time with him, and they all seemed cool." I reach over, touching my hand to his, and he flips his over, lacing our fingers together. "If they weren't okay with Bruce being out, they could have said something to me instead of having him picked up."

"Maybe it wasn't one of them. Maybe it was someone else," I suggest.

"Yeah, maybe. But what the fuck happened to his collar?"

"I don't know." I look back at Bruce, who's lying down on the bench seat. "The important thing is he's okay."

"You're right, but I need to have a fence put in and do it quickly. I don't want something like this happening again."

"I know you're busy with work, so I can make some calls today if you want. I know a few people in our neighborhood have had fencing put in recently. I can find out who they used and set up a time for them to give you an estimate."

"Better and fucking better," he mutters, looking at the windshield.

"What?"

"You." He glances at me quickly. "You just keep getting better and better." My heart thumps hard, and my hand in his spasms. "I'd really appreciate you doing that, baby."

"It's not a big deal."

He makes an *mmm-hmm* sound but doesn't say more.

When we get to his house, we take Bruce in, give him some food and water, and then track down Mouse, who decided to fall asleep in the top of Tyler's closet on a stack of his shirts. After I gather my stuff from last night, Tyler walks me over to my house, carrying Mouse for me with Bruce coming along. He leaves me at my front door with a swift kiss and a promise to see me later—most likely much later, because he's going to have to make up the hours from this morning. I reassure him that it's okay and that I'll take Bruce home, and then I'll get him when I get off work. I watch him through the window as he goes to his truck and backs out of his driveway, and only then do I go get myself ready for the day.

～

Standing in front of the tag machine in Petco with a new collar for Bruce in the bag hanging from my elbow, I type in his name, along with Tyler's information. I didn't tell Tyler that I would take care of this today, but I don't want Bruce going outside without a collar and tag. As the machine starts to engrave his name into the metal dog bone–shaped tag, I pull out my phone, snap a picture, and text it to Tyler.

"Leah?" At the sound of someone calling my name, I turn my head. "I thought that was you. I wasn't sure. Your hair is longer," my ex, Chris, says, smiling at me from a few feet away. "You look great. Well, you always look great, but I really like the longer hair."

"Uh . . . thanks."

He's still handsome, with dark reddish-brown hair, strong features, and a body he's built from years of swimming and running. I drop my eyes and see he has a pink leash in his grasp with a small white, fluffy dog wearing a black sweater with pink writing on it that claims she's a sweetheart.

"You got a dog?" I ask.

He laughs. "No, she's my girlfriend's. I was just picking her up from the groomer in the back."

"Awesome," I say as the machine beeps, letting me know the engraving is complete.

"You have a dog?"

"Yes. Well, my boyfriend does."

"I see." He nods, shoving his hands into the front pockets of his jeans. "How have you been? It's been forever."

"I've been really good, and you?" Do we really need to do this small talk business?

"I've been good." His eyes roam over me, making me feel awkward. "It's actually funny seeing you. I was just thinking about you the other day. We should have lunch sometime to catch up."

"I don't think we should," I reply, and he frowns.

"Why not?"

"First, I don't think we have anything to talk about, and second, I don't think my boyfriend would be okay with me having lunch with an ex." Actually, I *know* Tyler wouldn't, just from his reaction to the whole Charles situation.

"We were friends."

"Would your girlfriend be okay with you having lunch with me?"

"She wouldn't have a say in the matter."

"I see." My muscles get tight with annoyance.

"You see?" He frowns.

"I see that you haven't changed. Are you leading her on as well? Making her believe there's something serious between you when there isn't?"

"I never led you on." He pulls his hands from his pockets, his posture turning defensive.

"Oh yeah, you did. I will agree I let myself be sucked into the good times so deeply that I ignored most of the other crap you put me through, but yes, you did lead me on. You said you wanted to be with me, but you didn't really want me. You wanted me to want you, and then you wanted to have the option to do what you're doing right now." I wave my hand between us. "You wanted to be able to check and see if there was something else available to you, something you might think is better than what you have." I tip my head to the side. "It's smart, really. You get to go about your business without feeling guilty, while the person you're leading on is trying to come to terms with why they aren't good enough for you to commit to them."

He opens his mouth, but I continue talking. "I really hope you grow up. You're what? Forty-one, forty-two now? Pretty soon your charm is going to wear off, and you're not going to be as attractive. No woman is going to think dealing with your brand of bullshit is worth it when that happens."

With that, I snatch the dog tag from the slot in the machine and walk right past him out of the store. I get into my car, feeling totally and completely free, like a weight I didn't know I was carrying is now gone. I wanted to tell him all that when we were together, but I was never brave enough to say what I needed to say, because I didn't want to lose him. Now I see there was nothing to lose. Whoever that dog belongs to, I really hope she sees the kind of man he is a lot quicker than I did.

"You didn't." Chrissie laughs loudly, tossing her head back.

"I totally did. Besides, he had it coming. He was picking up his current girlfriend's dog and asking me to meet up with him. He's a douche."

"He really is." She sobers. "What did he expect? You to agree to meet with him, even after everything that happened between the two of you?"

"He thinks he's all that and can do whatever he wants without consequence. In his mind, he never really says he's committed, so he's free to do whatever he wants with whoever he wants."

"He's an idiot and a jerk."

"That he is," I agree. "I feel bad for his current girlfriend. If I knew who she was, I would tell her she needs to scrape him off and find someone who's worth her time."

"Enough about Chris. Tell me about you and Tyler," she says with a wide smile.

I filled her in as best I could over the phone about Tyler and me after she called me to say she'd heard about what had happened at the salon with Charles. I couldn't get into too much detail because I was still at work, but I promised her that I'd have her over for wine as long as she brought me cupcakes, which brings us to now. She and I are sitting at my kitchen table with Bruce lying at our feet and Mouse hiding somewhere in my house.

"We're together." I give a small smile. "I really like him. He's . . ." I pull in a breath, trying to figure out how to describe exactly what he is while I peel the paper off one of her chocolate-on-chocolate cupcakes and lift it to my mouth. "He's too good to be true. He's more than anything I've ever even hoped for in a guy." I take a bite of the cupcake and moan as the chocolate cream melts on my tongue.

"I'm happy for you." She grins. "I'm really happy you're finally seeing a guy who's worth your time."

"Me too," I agree after I chew and swallow. "But I keep thinking he's too good to be true, that at any moment he's going to show me who he really is, and I'm going to realize he's just like every other guy out there."

"He asked you to spend Thanksgiving with him and his family, babe. I don't think you have anything to worry about," she says softly, picking up a cupcake and licking off the icing.

"Do you think that maybe this is going too fast?" There are times I question our relationship, times I wonder if we're moving too quickly. Maybe we should slow down and take more time to get to know each other before spending every second together.

"No!" she practically shouts. "If a guy like him was interested in me, I'd be designing my wedding cake, sending out save the dates, and reserving a church for our wedding." I smile around a mouthful of chocolate cake. "I met him, babe. Any other guy, I might be concerned you were both moving too quickly, but I'm not worried about you with him. He seems sure, solid. I like him, and I really like how into you he is." She inhales deeply, then continues. "He couldn't keep his hands off you. Even when you thought you were just friends, he didn't stop touching you or talking to you softly. And the way he looked at you when you weren't paying attention—I swear I would pay for a guy to look at me like that."

"How did he look at me?" My heart starts to beat hard.

"Like he couldn't believe his luck, like he couldn't believe you were real and right there with him."

"He didn't look at me like that." We weren't even together then; we hadn't even kissed.

"He did, and everyone saw it. Even your mom made a comment when you two took off. She said that she was happy that a man was finally seeing what she's seen in you your whole life. A girl who deserves to have the world handed to her and to be protected."

"My mom said that?"

"She did."

Wow.

"It's scary," I whisper.

"What is?"

"I know I could fall in love with him. I can actually feel it happening with every moment we spend together, and there's nothing I can do to fight it. It's like it's inevitable, like no matter what I say or do, it's going to happen."

"That's not a bad thing," she says gently.

"No, I guess you're right. It's still scary, though, because I want this to work out so badly that I can actually taste it, and I know if it doesn't, I'm going to be crushed."

"That sounds pretty serious."

"I really like him, Chrissie. No—I more than like him. He makes me feel safe and wanted. He makes me feel beautiful. He makes me feel things I've never felt before with anyone. Plus, he's sweet, funny, protective, and possessive, and all of those things make me feel secure about what we're building. And I want to keep building on all of that. I don't want anything to ruin it, and I'm freaked that it really is too good to be true and that there's no way this is really happening."

"You might be overthinking things, Leah. Maybe you should just take it one day at a time and let him lead the way. He seems like he's good at leading, so you should let him do that." She grins.

I feel my face heat, knowing just how good he is at leading. "You're probably right."

"If I had any doubts about him, I'd tell you to slow down and guard your heart."

She would do that. She told me to be careful the first time Chris told me he wasn't sure about us, but like any good girlfriend, she was still supportive and hoped things would work out for me. When they didn't, she brought over wine and chocolate and let me cry on her shoulder. She never once said *I told you so*, even though she could have.

She wraps her hand around mine, which brings my attention back to her.

"I really do believe that he is who he says he is. I think he's exactly what you said earlier—sweet, funny, and totally into you."

"I really hope so," I say, and just as I do, Bruce lifts his head. I hear the front door open, and Bruce gets up off the floor, rushing with his tail wagging and claws tapping the hardwood as he runs for his dad. I smile, because I know Tyler is home, and Chrissie grins at me from across my small table.

"I should go." She starts to stand, but I stop her, keeping my hand wrapped around hers and holding her in place. I don't want her to go. I miss spending time with her and really want her to get to know Tyler. I never wanted that before—her to get to know anyone I was with.

"Stay for dinner."

She laughs. "Leah, babe, it's eight. My dinner tonight consisted of good conversation, wine, and cupcakes. If I eat any more, I won't be able to fit in my jeans tomorrow."

"Crap." I look at the clock to confirm she's right. I lost track of time and didn't even think about Tyler coming home after working all day and being hungry. "I suck as a girlfriend," I state, my shoulders slumping.

"Why's that?" Tyler asks, resting his hand on my shoulder, and I tip my head back to look at him. I notice that he has a bag in hand, and from the scent of curry wafting from it, it's Indian food.

"I didn't make dinner," I tell him, and he bends over, giving me an upside-down kiss that rivals the one in *Spider-Man*, because it leaves me completely breathless.

"You sent a text. I knew Chrissie was here, so I brought dinner. I figured wine and cake wouldn't cut it." He glances at the four cupcakes still sitting on the table in a light-yellow box. "Though, from the small taste I just got, those are gonna be good."

"They're delicious," I tell him, and he grins at me, then lifts his head.

"Hey, Chrissie."

"Tyler."

I know by the sound of her voice that if I look at my friend's face, I'll see my own look reflected back at me. Total and complete awe, because men like him aren't real.

"I got enough food for the three of us. I hope you'll stay for dinner, even though it's late."

"I'll stay," she agrees instantly, the thought of fitting into her jeans tomorrow long gone in the presence of my man.

"Good." He gives her a smile and me another upside-down kiss, this one shorter than the one before. He lets me go and heads for the counter, where he drops the bag. "Thanks, baby, for getting Bruce's tag and new collar."

"No biggie." At my statement, his expression warms, and I swear I feel that warmth seeping into every cell in my body as I look into his eyes across the space between us.

He shakes his head. "Right. I'll let you two sort out dinner while I take Bruce out with me. I need to stop at my place, get the mail, and grab some stuff for tomorrow." He comes back toward me in his boots, jeans, and long-sleeve shirt with a vest over it. "Be back in ten or fifteen."

"Okay." I know my voice is breathy as he touches his mouth to mine again. He heads for the doorway in the kitchen, calling out to Bruce as he disappears from sight, and Bruce follows after coming to get an ear scratch from me.

"I better be your bridesmaid, and no matter what you say, I get to design your cake," Chrissie demands. I look at her and start to laugh. "I'm serious," she states, standing and placing her hands on her hips to emphasize her point.

"I wouldn't have anyone else for either job," I assure her while getting up myself and heading for the counter where the food is.

"Have I told you I love him for you?"

"You might have mentioned it." I smile at her from across the counter as she picks up our empty wineglasses.

"Well, let me reiterate the point, because I really, really love him for you."

With that final statement from my best friend, I serve us up dinner. When Tyler gets back, the three of us eat sitting at my small table, laughing and talking. I cannot imagine a more perfect evening. Not only am I able to enjoy the company of my best friend, but I also get to share my happiness with the guy who is slowly winning over my heart.

Suggestion 9

Don't Let A Little Arson Ruin Your Night

LEAH

"Shit," I hear Tyler say as I walk out of my bedroom. I hit the living room, and his eyes land on me. The anger I saw when I entered disintegrates as his gaze licks over me from head to toe, and something else fills his eyes. That something is so hot my toes curl and my body tingles.

It's Saturday, and we're going on our first real date, which is why I'm wearing the new red dress I bought yesterday. A deep bloodred dress with a tie at the waist, a low neck that shows off my cleavage, and a hem hitting just below my knees. I've complemented the look with high-heeled black suede boots that come to midthigh. As anger and frustration fill his gaze once more, I notice he has his phone to his ear.

"Yeah, fuck, I'll be there. I just need to explain to Leah what's going on." He pauses, and his lips slightly lift at the corners. "You'll meet her soon, just need to set up a time to do that," he says, and I kinda tune him out after that, because I'm taking in all of him. He's wearing black dress shoes I'm surprised he owns (because I've never seen him in anything but work boots), nice belted slacks, and a dark-blue fitted button-down shirt that had to have been tailored just for him, since it fits that well. My body doesn't just tingle; it heats up, sending a surge of want and desire through me.

I stop thinking about taking off his clothes and having my way with him when his hand curls around my hip, the other curving around my neck.

"Jesus, baby, you're fucking amazing." He growls those words, which sends a pulse between my legs. I lift my hands to his chest, digging into his shirt and flesh with the tips of my fingers to steady myself. "I'm sorry."

Wait, what is he sorry about?

"Sorry?" I focus on him, and he moves his face closer to mine.

"I gotta leave. There was a fire in one of our off-site storage spaces. Scott is there now, along with the police and fire department. They think an accelerant was used, which means it could be arson."

"Was anyone hurt?" I ask in worry.

He shakes his head. "No one was there, and the place isn't in a residential area. All that's on the property is a metal building and a big dirt lot surrounded by a fence."

"You said they think it might be arson?"

"That's what the police and fire department are saying, which is why Scott wants me there with him."

"Why would someone do that?" I ask, searching his eyes.

"Who knows? Maybe one of the people competing for the bid on the hotel got pissed they lost and wants to run us off so they can do the job themselves. Or maybe an ex-employee is out for revenge." He tightens his hold on me when unease slides down my spine. "It could be none of that and just someone being a dick, baby, so get that look out of your eyes."

"Okay," I agree reluctantly.

"Now, I really, really hate that I have to leave right now, especially when I want nothing more than to strip that dress off your beautiful body, explore what you've got under it, and then fuck you in those boots."

"Tyler." My voice is raspy as I settle my weight deeper against him.

"I don't know how long this is gonna take, baby, so we're gonna have to postpone our dinner plans for the night."

I hate that we have to do that, but I understand. "Will you ask me out again?" I ask, and his eyes lock with mine and light up.

"Fuck yeah."

"Then it's okay." I get up on my tiptoes and softly press my lips to his. "I still have something to look forward to."

"Fuck, I—" His words are cut off when his cell phone rings. I settle back to my flat feet, and he groans. "I'll be back here as soon as this shit is sorted."

"I'll be waiting," I tell him.

He presses his mouth hard against mine and lets me go, putting his phone to his ear. I listen to him clip out, "Yeah, on my way," before he opens the door, locks it from the inside, and steps out. I stand in the middle of my living room for a long time wondering what he was going to say, and then eventually I get myself together and come up with a plan. Our date night might have gone up in smoke, but the night isn't over yet.

I make a call and then get in my car. When I get back home, I set things up, but one thing I don't do is take off my dress before I settle on the couch to wait.

"Baby," I hear Tyler's voice whisper against my ear while fingers trail down the side of my face and neck and along the edge of my breast.

Blinking my eyes open, I find his face so close to mine that I can see a small speckle in his right eye that I hadn't noticed before now. "You're home."

His expression gentles, and he leans back slightly where he's sitting on my coffee table. "Yeah, but baby, I wish you didn't wait up. You're tired; you fell asleep on the couch still wearing your dress."

At the mention of my dress, sleep leaves me instantly, replaced with something else. "I'm okay," I assure him while I sit up. "Can you wait here a second?" I ask after I get up off the couch and look down at him.

"Sure."

I feel him watching me as I leave the living room and go through the kitchen doorway. I pull out the dinner I ordered us, heat it in the microwave, and light the two candles I placed in the middle of the table. Once I have our plates ready, I shut off the overhead light and let the candlelight take me back to him. I grasp his hand and lead him to the kitchen, where I covered the table in a white cloth. I set the table for two with the robin's-egg-blue-and-gold place settings my grams gave to me as a housewarming gift. She told me to use them for special occasions. I never had one until tonight.

"Baby." His voice is rough as he takes a seat, and I sit across from him.

"I know this wasn't exactly what we had planned," I start, and his gaze lifts from the plate in front of him to meet mine. "But I hope it's okay."

"This is better than okay, beautiful. This is—"

"Our first real date, just in a different location," I state, picking up my wineglass, which is filled halfway with water.

With his eyes still on mine, he nods and then picks up his glass of water and holds it out between us. "Here's to a lot more firsts."

I smile as I tap my glass to his. I cut into the orange chicken I ordered, then take a bite. This isn't the steak I know he probably would have ordered tonight, but steak doesn't taste as good reheated.

As we sit across from each other, I don't ask him what happened, and he doesn't tell me. We just enjoy each other's company, and when we're finished, he takes me to the bedroom, where he does exactly what he described earlier. He removes my dress and explores the lacy red undergarments I have on underneath, and then he fucks me with my boots still on. It's the perfect first date and a night I will remember until I take my last breath.

～

"Coffee?" Tyler asks, and I nod grumpily at him, wondering how on earth he can be so happy at six in the morning. Normal people aren't happy until at least eight, and even then, that's only after consuming a ton of coffee. "Baby, I've told you before you don't gotta get up with me when I get up for work." He pours me a cup of coffee, adds milk and sugar, and slides it toward me across the counter.

"You didn't exactly let me sleep in," I remind him as I wrap both hands around the cup and lift it to my mouth.

"Maybe if you didn't fall asleep completely naked, I would've been able to control myself. I didn't have any self-control. I was already deep inside you when I woke up," he lies with a shrug.

"Whatever," I grumble. I'm not going to complain about him waking me like he did when I totally enjoyed every second, including the shower we shared afterward. I catch his smile as he turns to the stove. He slides two eggs and sliced Spam from the skillet onto a plate for himself. I might be up and drinking coffee with him, but he knows in no way am I ready to start my day with a big breakfast.

"What's on your schedule for the day?" he asks.

Since he finished with the church last week, he's been working at the hotel with just a few of his men, getting things ready for the renovation while they wait for the new supplies they had to order after the fire. He told me that the fire marshal concluded it was arson after he found a black trail that led to a melted gasoline can just inside the door of the building. The building is still partially standing, but the contents they'd stored inside—wood, paint, carpet, anything and everything you'd use during a renovation—were destroyed either by the fire itself or by smoke or water damage.

Scott, whom I met a few days ago when he came to drop off paperwork, was not happy about what happened, but since he had insurance to cover the cost of the things that were lost, he wasn't as devastated as he could have been. The police still have no suspects, but they did get a partial print off the gas can. They aren't very hopeful they'll be able to find the person responsible with the print alone, but they're still looking at a list of suspects Tyler and Scott came up with. I really hope they find whoever set the fire. If that fire had happened anywhere else, homes could have been destroyed and lives could have been lost.

"Baby, go back to bed. You're sleeping on your feet." Tyler touches my face gently, and I focus on him.

"Sorry, I spaced." I take a sip of coffee, then remember his earlier question and think about the fact it's Monday. "I have a doctor's appointment at noon."

"Doctor's appointment?" He takes a bite of eggs and Spam.

I feel my cheeks get warm, which is ridiculous, since we've talked about this. We talked about it the first time we screwed up and didn't use protection. From that conversation, I found out he hadn't been with anyone for a long time before me and is clean—thankfully. And he knows I am as well, but since then we've had sex several more times without a condom, so lost in the moment we didn't think about it.

As happy as I am to be with him, this isn't a good time to test fate. We don't need a baby, not right now, not while we're really just getting to know each other.

"I'm seeing my doctor about birth control," I say quietly.

"Shit," he mutters. "I didn't think this morning. I—"

I cut him off. "You're not the only one." It's not all on him; I should have thought about it, too, but I didn't. "Hopefully, after today we won't have to think about it again."

"I should have protected you." He reaches out and takes my hand in his. "You're the first woman who's ever made me so fucking hot and so fucking hard I stop thinking about everything but being inside you, connecting with you." He shakes his head like he's trying to get rid of the thought. "I'll be more careful until you tell me we're good."

Can he be any more perfect? I doubt it, seriously.

"Thank you. That means everything," I whisper, my emotions too high to speak any louder.

"Just so you know, baby, if we did make a child, I wouldn't regret it for a second, not one goddamn second."

My heart feels funny in my chest as I stare into his eyes. I know I'm not just falling for him; I've already fallen. I love this man. He's every hope, dream, and wish wrapped up in the perfect man. Sure, he still makes me a little crazy from time to time, but I like that he does. I don't think I would feel this way about him if he didn't.

I want so badly to tell him that I love him, but I'm not sure right now is the time to admit something so huge. Not with him having to leave for work in just a few minutes. "Tyler—"

He cuts me off. "Tonight we're going out. I don't give a fuck about work or whatever else we have going on. I'm taking my girl out to dinner."

"Are you asking me on a date or telling me we're going on one?" I quip, and he grins.

"Take it how you want, baby, but we're going out tonight." He lets my hand go and takes another bite off his plate.

"So you're telling, then." I smile like an idiot.

He finishes his food, takes a sip of coffee, and then leans across the counter. He kisses me, tangling his fingers in my hair to hold me to him as he devours my mouth. When he lets me go, I let out a small sad whimper. "Wear a dress. I should be here at five thirty."

"Got it," I breathe out, and he smiles, then lets me go completely. He rinses his plate and puts it in the dishwasher, along with his coffee mug. When he comes back, he walks around the counter, drags me up out of my seat, and kisses me again before he releases me, says goodbye to Bruce, and takes off. I sit in my kitchen for a long time sipping coffee before I decide I'm going back to bed. I don't have to work until ten, so I can still get a few more hours of sleep.

"Since you're here and you're due for your yearly checkup, I thought, if you're okay with it, we could take care of your yearly physical and Pap smear today," my doctor says with a smile. I have no idea what she's smiling about. I hate this part of being a woman, hate lying on a cold piece of plastic covered with paper to be examined by someone I hardly know.

"Sure," I agree, even though I don't want to. I feel like I need more time to prepare for this, like it's a pop quiz I didn't have a chance to study for.

"All right, just pee in this cup and leave it in the little slot in the restroom." She hands me a small cup and two wipes. "Change into this when you come back." She hands me a folded gown. "After I get the results from your urine test and confirm you're not pregnant, I'll come back in and examine you, then write the prescription for your birth control."

After I go to the bathroom and take care of business, I take a seat on the examination table and cringe as the paper that covers it crackles loudly in the quiet room. It seems to take forever for my doctor to come back, and when she does, she comes in with a nurse. She tells me that I'm not pregnant, then has me lie back on the table.

After she's done with my exam, I sit up, and she gives me a run-down about the pill. She tells me the warning signs I need to look out for, then explains that Tyler and I need to be careful for the next month until my hormones adjust and to be sure to use condoms. But if either of us is having sex with anyone else, we should keep using condoms, she says, because birth control doesn't protect against sexually transmitted diseases.

After she leaves the room, I get dressed. I have a client scheduled for two—a quick cut and blowout—and another client at three, who's getting partial highlights. I should have plenty of time after my last client to go home and get ready for my date with Tyler. When I get in my car, I check my phone when it beeps and smile when I see a message from him on the screen.

Tyler: How was your appointment?

I message back quickly after starting my car to warm it up. The temperature has dropped in the last few days, and it's close to freezing outside. I even had to pull out my big down jacket this morning.

Me: It went good. Let the countdown to no more condoms begin. ;)

Tyler: Looking forward to that baby. I'll see you in a few hours have a good day.

Me: You too.

I drop my phone into the cup holder and head for work. When I arrive, I greet both Mom and Grams with kisses to their cheeks, then get things ready for my afternoon appointments. Work flies by in a flash, and when it's done, I head home. I park in my garage and go into the house, where I set down food for Mouse before leaving through the front door and rushing to get Bruce. He and Mouse seem to get along, but I'm not brave enough to leave the two of them alone in my place while I'm at work.

I let myself into Tyler's house and call out to Bruce as soon as I step inside. He rushes toward me with his tail wagging and body shaking in excitement. "Hey, big guy." I rub the top of his head while I squat to attach the leash to his collar. The fencing company won't be able to start work for another week, which means until then, Bruce isn't allowed to go out without someone with him.

"Leah." When a woman says my name, I jump in place with my heart lodged in my throat. My head flies up as a woman I don't know comes toward me. "I'm guessing you're Leah, since I don't think my brother would give his key to just anyone. Plus, Bruce seems to know you."

Oh my God. Tyler's sister? I didn't know she was going to be coming to town. Tyler mentioned a few days ago that his sister was divorcing and going through a serious custody battle with her soon-to-be-ex-husband, but he didn't mention she'd be here.

"Heather?" She's a prettier version of Tyler, with long dark hair cut into lots of layers, big blue eyes that take up most of her face, and an hourglass figure of which I'm instantly envious. Wearing cowboy boots, wide-leg jeans, and a button-down plaid shirt, she looks like she belongs on a farm in Tennessee.

"I see he's told you about me as well." She comes toward me, and I stand just in time for her to wrap her arms around me in a hug.

"I . . ." I pause when she lets me go, then shake my head. "Tyler didn't tell me you were coming to town."

"He didn't know." She smiles softly, taking a step back. "Kennedy and I needed a little break from Montana, so I thought I'd surprise my little brother with a visit."

"Kennedy is here?" I ask, looking around for Tyler's adorable nine-month-old niece I've seen pictures and videos of on his phone.

Her face softens. "Yeah, but she's sleeping. She passed out after we got here. I laid her down in Tyler's room."

"He's going to be so happy to see you both." I don't tell her that he's been worried about them. I don't think that's something she needs a reminder of right now. From what Tyler's said, her divorce has been ugly and the fight for custody even worse.

"Hopefully, that's true. I know he wasn't expecting us. I called him earlier, but he didn't answer. I wanted to give him a little heads-up, but I know he's working."

"He won't care," I assure her, and then I look down at Bruce, who licks my hand. "I'll take him out if you haven't already. Then I'll come back here and hang with you until your brother gets off work, if that's okay with you."

"I didn't have a chance to take him out, but I'd really like to hang with you when you get back," she agrees with a grin.

"Cool." I smile in return, then lead Bruce outside and take him on a short walk to take care of business. On the way back, I stop at my house to get my cell phone and send Tyler a text letting him know I'll be at his house. When I get back to his house, Kennedy is awake, and she's just as adorable in person as she seemed to be in photos.

Stretched out on a blanket on Tyler's floor, Kennedy crawls toward me and the toy duck I'm waving at her. She gurgles and smiles, and I laugh. I pick her up and lift her above my head, laughing with her as she giggles. There's nothing better than a baby's laugh. The carefree sound they make is irreplaceable. I miss when my niece and nephews were this age. I miss the way they looked at the world with complete wonder. I tuck Kennedy to my chest and then kiss the top of her head and smile at her mom, who's sitting on the couch watching us.

"You're good with kids," Heather says with a smile.

"I have a niece and two nephews. They're older now, and most of the time they're running away from being cuddled by their aunt," I tell her while laughing as Kennedy fights to get away from my hug. Once she's free, she wraps her hands around my fingers and stands while bouncing up and down on my thighs. "I miss when they were this age."

"Do you want kids of your own one day?" she asks, watching us.

"Yes." I bend forward and blow a raspberry on Kennedy's neck, making her giggle. "I want a dozen of these adorable bundles of joy."

"A dozen?" Her eyes widen, and I laugh.

"Okay, maybe three or four, tops, but I've always wanted to be a mom. I always wanted to cook dinners, do craft projects and homework, and take care of little ones," I tell her, watching Kennedy smile and drool while bouncing.

"Tyler's always wanted kids," she says, and I look up to find her studying me. "He's always been about family."

I know that, even without him telling me. I can see it in his eyes when he talks about his parents and sister. I know how much he loves them, how much his family means to him. I know he'll be an amazing dad one day, because he's great with my niece and nephews and proud to be an uncle.

"I didn't think—"

Heather's words are cut off when Tyler comes through the front door. His gaze lands on me first, and confusion fills his eyes before he sees his sister. Then happiness settles into his features.

"What are you doing here?" he asks with a wide smile as Heather rushes across the room and into his arms. I watch the two of them embrace, rocking from side to side. Kennedy screeches loudly, not wanting to be left out of the reunion, so I pick her up and take her to her mom and uncle. "Hey, little one," Tyler whispers, touching her cheek when he locks eyes with his niece.

Instead of going to Tyler, she wiggles out of my arms and latches on to her mom, tucking her face into Heather's neck. Tyler laughs and wraps his arms around the three of us. I feel something deep within my heart fill during the embrace. This is what I want, except I want to feel Tyler wrapped around me and our kids one day. I want to feel his strong arms surrounding us as we welcome him home from work. I want a lifetime of this feeling.

"How long are you here for?" he asks once he's let his sister and niece go, and then he wraps his arm around my shoulders.

"Just through the weekend. I wanted to see you since I won't be able to get away for Thanksgiving," Heather says, seeming to tighten her hold on Kennedy, like she might disappear.

"He's not letting you leave for the holiday?" Tyler guesses, and Heather nods. "Dick."

I feel his anger like a physical thing beating against me. I rest my hand against his stomach and look up at him. I hate how upset he looks, and I hate worse there's nothing I can do to change it.

"Are you hungry?" I ask Heather, wanting to change the subject and, hopefully, the mood in the room. After she nods, I tell her, "There's a great Mexican place near here. Do you like Mexican food?"

"I love Mexican food." She goes to the couch, and I see her pick up a small bag covered in flowers and lay Kennedy down on a mat.

I look up at Tyler. "You should take them to eat."

"You're coming with us."

"Are you sure? I don't want to intrude, and maybe you two need some time alone."

"I appreciate you saying that, baby, but I want you with us. I want you to get to know my sister while she's here."

"If that's what you want," I agree quietly.

"It's what I want." He touches his mouth to mine in a short kiss. "I'm going to change. When I get done, we'll head out."

"Sounds good." He gives me a squeeze before walking off, and I watch him go. I ask Heather, "Do you want me to help with anything for Kennedy?"

"No, I'm used to doing it on my own." She smiles at me, and I hate that is something she's used to. Being a single parent isn't easy, but being a single parent when you're in a relationship must be worse.

"I can make a bottle," I tell her, picking up a half-empty one from the coffee table.

"It's okay. She had one not long ago, and I have travel formula packs. I'll just bring those and a jar of her food with us and feed her at the restaurant."

"Okay," I agree, watching her change Kennedy's diaper and put her in a different outfit, one warmer than the simple onesie she had on before. I take the bottle in my hand to the kitchen and rinse it, then place it in the sink.

"Do you mind holding her while I go to the bathroom?" Heather asks once she's standing with Kennedy in her arms.

"Not at all." I hold out my hands as she reaches for me. I place her on my hip and look down at her sweet little face before looking at her mom. "She'll be okay."

"Thanks." She leaves and heads down the back hallway. I watch her go, then take a seat on the couch, laughing as Kennedy tries to eat my hair and drools on me in the process.

"Is Heather changing?" Tyler asks. He appears at the edge of the couch wearing different jeans and a long-sleeve henley.

"Using the bathroom." I smile as he takes a seat next to us.

Kennedy loses interest in my hair and lunges for her uncle, who easily accepts the burden of her wiggling body. "She seems off," he states quietly, and I know he's talking about his sister.

"I don't know her, but I think you're right," I whisper back. "This weekend, you should find time to talk with her alone. If you want, I'll watch Kennedy. Maybe she'll open up about things with you."

"I think that'd be good," he agrees. I lean into his side and watch him play with his niece. When Heather comes back, we all go out to dinner. It's not the date we'd planned for tonight, but then again, it's better, because I get to spend time with Tyler and his family.

Suggestion 10

Do Not Panic

LEAH

My front door opens, and Tyler walks in with Heather right behind him. I smile from where I'm lounging on the couch with Kennedy, who's asleep on her stomach. I have a stack of pillows built into a wall to prevent her from rolling off. "How was lunch?" I ask quietly as Tyler greets me with a kiss.

"Good, baby, thanks for looking after Kennedy."

I nod at him.

"Was she okay?" Heather asks, looking down at her sleeping girl.

"She was perfect. I gave her a bottle about an hour ago, and she fell asleep right after she burped."

Her eyes come to me, and I see tears shimmer in them. "Thank you."

"Anytime, seriously. I loved spending time with her," I say softly.

I watch her inhale deeply and nod, and then she looks at her brother. "You can go make out with her now," she says, and I start to laugh, and Tyler chuckles as I get up off the couch. She takes my seat and rests her hand on Kennedy's bottom; she's lounging on her side with her eyes on the TV.

The last couple of days, she has caught Tyler and I making out more than once. It's not that we're trying to hide our relationship; we just don't want what we're building to be in her face, especially with what she's going through. Since Tyler only has one bed at his place, he gave it to his sister and has been sleeping with me at my place. Not that that's new—he was staying with me before she arrived.

"Be back in a minute," Tyler says, taking my hand and pulling me with him to the kitchen.

"How did it go?" I ask softly once we're out of earshot of the living room.

"She opened up," he tells me, running his fingers through his hair. "He's going for full custody, and unlike my sister, he has the resources to back him up."

I get closer to him and rest my hands against his chest. "I don't know much about this kind of thing, but aren't mothers normally granted custody?"

"Maybe." He shrugs. "But her soon-to-be-ex-husband owns one of the biggest logging companies in Montana. He grew up there and knows everyone. She's worried he will win, and she's right to worry about it."

"It will be okay."

"I'm not sure it will, but I told her she should consider moving back to Tennessee after everything is said and done. She didn't like that idea but said she might consider moving here."

"I'd like that."

Heather is just as laid back and easy to get along with as her brother. Plus, Kennedy is adorable, and I've loved spending time with both of them over the last few days.

"I want her away from him and that town. I wish she'd never met that fucking guy and moved away," he says harshly.

"If that hadn't happened, there wouldn't be any Kennedy. And I know you can't imagine a world without her. I agree Heather's struggling right now, but she seems pretty damn strong. She'll be okay. Maybe not today or a month from now, but she will be okay eventually. And hopefully, when the smoke clears, she'll be moving here."

"Fuck." His arms wrap around me tightly. "Jesus, I love you." I freeze, my whole body tightening along with my lungs. Did he tell me he loves me because he's in love with me, or was it more of a *You said what I needed to hear, and I love you for that?* "I know you might not be there yet, but I need you to know that I love you, Leah. You're the best thing that has ever happened to me."

My eyes slide closed, and my body relaxes against his as happiness fills me. "I love you too." The words come out so softly that I wonder if he was even able to hear them.

He pulls his head back and looks down at me, capturing my face between his palms. "Say it again," he demands on a soft growl.

I feel tears begin to build as I look at him. "I love you, Tyler."

He rests his forehead against mine, and I see him smile before he mutters, "Thank fuck."

I laugh, and he chuckles right before he kisses me. When his tongue sweeps into my mouth, I hold on to him as tightly as I can and kiss him back. In just a few short weeks, he's changed everything. He's shown me that it's okay to fall if you're falling for the right person, and he's made me believe that my own happily ever after is possible.

"Sorry," Heather says, and Tyler pulls his mouth from mine and tucks my face into his neck.

"You good?" he asks, and I turn my head against his chest to look at his sister, standing in the doorway of the kitchen.

"Mom called me. She said she tried to reach you, but you didn't answer." She shifts, looking slightly uncomfortable.

I feel his arms around me tighten, and then I tip my head back when he groans. "Fuck, I'll call her."

"Is everything okay?" I ask, and he looks down at me. I swear I think he looks worried, but I don't know what he could be worried about.

"Everything's fine. I just need to call her back. I'll do it while I take Bruce out."

"Sure," I agree, and he lets me go and grabs Bruce's leash, which is hanging on the handle of the pantry door in my kitchen.

"Be right back," he tells Heather and me before he disappears.

"Is everything with your parents okay?" I question when I hear the front door open and shut.

Heather presses her lips together, looking unsure, and then she lets out a breath and relaxes them before answering. "Our mom wasn't really happy about Tyler leaving town, the same way she wasn't happy about me moving to Montana. She's been trying for a while to convince Tyler to come home. I think with you in the picture, she knows that's not going to happen."

"Oh." What do I say to that? Tyler never told me that his mom isn't happy about him living here. I get it—I don't think my mom would be happy about me moving to another state, even as old as I am.

"She'll come around eventually."

"We're going to Tennessee for Thanksgiving. Hopefully, her seeing him will help," I say.

She nods but doesn't look convinced. "Just don't let her get to you. She can be a lot sometimes. Marvin had a hard time dealing with it in the beginning, and that took a toll on us."

"Now I'm worried," I admit, since she and her husband are currently in the middle of a divorce, and an ugly one at that.

"I probably shouldn't have said anything. I just don't want you to be caught off guard. I love my mom. She's great. But when she's not getting what she wants, she tends to play dirty."

My eyes are wide. Now not only am I worried, I'm freaked out. What the hell does that mean? "Play dirty?"

"Tyler will deal with her if she does anything," she assures me, and then we both look into the living room after Kennedy lets out a small cry.

She turns to go to her, so I don't get to question her any more about her mom. Really, I don't know that I want to know more than I do. What the hell have I gotten myself into? I wonder if I should make up some kind of excuse so I don't have to go with him, but then I think about Tyler telling me that he loves me, and I know I can't do that. He said he wants me to meet his family, and his mom can't be that bad. He loves her, and it's obvious Heather does too.

With a long sigh, I go to the living room and sit with Heather and Kennedy until Tyler gets back, and then we all load up and go to his place. Heather is leaving early tomorrow morning, so she needs to pack up and get ready for the long flight.

We have dinner together; Tyler makes lasagna, and Heather helps him while I spend time with Kennedy. When the night comes to an end, I say goodbye to Heather and Kennedy at Tyler's door. They're heading for the airport at four in the morning, so I won't see them again before they leave. After my goodbye, Tyler walks me to my house and tells me that he'll see me tomorrow. He's going to spend the night on the couch at his place so he can see his sister off. I hate that I don't get to sleep in his arms, but I understand.

When I get into my empty bed, which has never felt empty before, I hug Tyler's pillow to my chest, reminding myself that it's just one night. I'll see him in the morning, and I'll get to spend all day with him since he and I are going to my parents' for Sunday dinner.

It takes me forever to fall asleep, and when I do, I dream about an evil witch trying to chase me out of a castle. I wake earlier than normal and lie in bed for a long time, wondering if it was a vision of things to come.

Suggestion 11

GIVE HER WHAT SHE NEEDS

TYLER

I catch Leah smiling at me as I help her out of my truck, and then I take her hand.

"Have I told you how handsome you look in a baseball hat?" she says as I look down at her, my brows drawing together.

"What?"

"There's something about you wearing a baseball hat that does it for me. Especially when you wear it backward, which is something you don't do all the time." She scans my face. "You look hot."

I grin at her. "I'll remember that," I say before leading her up the walkway toward her parents' front door.

When we're halfway up the walk, she asks, "Have you heard from Heather yet?" The mention of my sister makes my gut tighten. I didn't want to let her and my niece leave this morning, not with everything happening in Montana. Like Leah said, she'll be okay eventually, but she's far from okay right now, and I hate that I can't protect her.

"She texted that she and Kennedy were in Seattle waiting to board a flight to Montana. She'll message once she hits Missoula."

Her face falls. "I wish she could have stayed and come to Sunday dinner with us. My mom would have loved her and Kennedy."

The tightness in my gut eases. Heather, like my mother, has never really gotten along with or approved of anyone I've dated. I love the bond Heather and Leah formed during her short stay. Not that I'm really surprised by it. Leah has a way of making you fall in love with her the moment you meet her.

"I hope there will be a time in the near future that inviting her to Sunday dinner can be a regular occurrence."

"I hope so too," she agrees, touching her fingers lightly to my jaw.

Like the miracle worker she is, she causes my body to relax completely. I thought I'd fallen in love before. But I realized that until Leah I'd never really experienced the soul-deep feeling of contentment and happiness that comes with true love. In a short amount of time, she's changed my whole world. She's changed my purpose in life. Before her I was focused on work, on my career; now I'm looking forward to the life we'll build together, the family we'll one day have.

Jesus, I want to pick her up and take her to bed and show her exactly what she means to me.

"Baby, how important is Sunday dinner to you?" I pull her against me while dropping my face to hers.

"Wh-what?" she stammers, scanning my eyes.

"I really want—"

"Are you two gonna stand outside or come on in?" her dad says as he opens the door suddenly, and I growl deep in my throat, aggravated by the intrusion.

Leah's eyes fly from mine to her father's, and she visibly swallows. "We . . . ," she starts, then glances at me once more. Her pupils are dilated, and her expression is filled with confusion.

"We're coming in," I say. As much as I want to cart her off, I know I shouldn't. She enjoys spending time with her family, and I actually do too. Plus, I get her all night after we leave here.

"Come inside, then." Her dad holds the door open for us. After hugs for Leah and a handshake for me, he tells us to take off our coats. We drop them on the back of the couch, where there'll be a pile later when the rest of the family arrives. Just like the first time I was here, Leah's father starts talking sports, and Leah zones out. I kiss her after she tells me she's going to check on her mom.

A few minutes later, she comes back out with two beers. She hands one to her dad and kisses his cheek before heading toward me.

"Are you okay?" she asks, holding out a beer but not letting it go.

"I'm good, baby." Her eyes search mine. I tug her down toward me and steal a quick kiss, causing her cheeks to turn an adorable shade of pink. I let her go instead of dragging her onto my lap like I want. "Do you and your mom need help in the kitchen?"

"No, she's pretty much got everything done."

"Do you wanna hang here and watch the game with me and your dad?" She glances at the TV and scrunches up her nose. "I'll take that as a no."

"Sorry." She shrugs with a goofy smile. I chuckle and accept a kiss from her before she leaves me alone with her father once more. When her brothers arrive a little later, she comes out of hiding so she can smother her niece and nephews with kisses and hugs. I love their relationship, and when I see her with them, I can imagine her as a mom, can see she'll have the same fun-loving, light relationship with her own children one day.

"So you're going to Tennessee for Thanksgiving?" Ben asks once we're all sitting around the table and have loaded our plates.

"Yep." Her eyes widen slightly. "Any advice for meeting Tyler's parents?"

"Don't talk," Ben says, and everyone laughs.

"I'll take Bruce if he's not going with you." Noah looks at me.

"Heck yeah," Owen shouts with a wide smile, and I look at him. I'd planned on taking Bruce with us, but after seeing Owen's excitement, I decide he'll stay behind this time.

"Thanks, man, I'd appreciate that."

"No worries." Noah shrugs.

The rest of the evening passes with great food and laughter and good conversation, but I still can't wait to get Leah to myself again. After we say goodbye to everyone, I put her in my truck and take her home, where I show her how much she means to me, using her body and mine to accomplish my goal.

"Sorry, man, can't get drinks tonight," I tell Scott. I'm holding my cell to my ear as I walk across the lot to my truck after work. "I'm taking Leah out to dinner. It's Friday and one of the only nights she and I have got before we head to Tennessee for Thanksgiving." I've been looking forward to this dinner since the fire and my sister showing up unexpectedly. I'm filled with anticipation about seeing just what she'll wear tonight and then planning exactly how I'll get her out of it after we get home. Just the thought makes my palms itch.

"I get it." I hear the smile in his tone. "When you get back, we'll meet up." After a few moments, he asks, "Are you gonna be okay being at home with your family? With them meeting Leah?" Scott and I have been friends since high school, so he knows how my mom can be. I despise the sudden feeling in my stomach. A feeling of unease that I shouldn't have when it comes to introducing my parents—mainly my mother—to the woman I've fallen in love with.

"Leah will be with me, so even if it's not okay, it will be okay." That's the truth. Leah has a way of centering me, of bringing me happiness.

"All right, man, let me know if you need anything."

"Will do—later."

"Yeah, later." He hangs up, and I get behind the wheel and reverse out of my parking spot. I pick up a dozen pink roses before I head home. Leah texted earlier to let me know Bruce was with her, which wasn't a surprise. He's become her loyal companion, and just like me, he fell for her quickly. When I get home, I shower and change, then head to Leah's house with the flowers in tow. She gave me her key a couple of weeks ago, so I let myself in, and Bruce greets me at the door. "Hey, buddy." I rub the top of his head. "Where's our girl?" He moves toward the hall as I head through the house, and I drop the flowers in the kitchen.

Leah's place doesn't have the same layout as mine. Where my living room and kitchen are one large open space, her living room is separated from her kitchen and dining room by curved archways leading to both spaces. Her two bedrooms are down a short hall, and she has a full basement that's unfinished except for a small room containing a washer and dryer.

Music is coming from Leah's bedroom. I push open the door and lean against the doorjamb, watching her bend at the waist to buckle the strap of one of her black suede heels. She stands, sliding her hands over her full hips, and the formfitting deep-blue sweater dress she has on shows off every curve. I bite back a groan as I take her in. *Jesus, she's beautiful.* She's always so damn beautiful, and it's hard to believe she's mine. When she sees me standing inside the doorway, she freezes, then bites the inside of her cheek as I walk toward her. When I'm close enough, I grab her hips and lower my face toward hers.

"You look beautiful."

"Thanks." She smiles bashfully, ducking her head. How a woman who looks like her can be bashful is mind boggling.

"Are you ready to go?"

"I just need to change out my purse." She looks up at me. "It'll only take a minute."

"All right." I kiss her forehead. "I'll meet you in the kitchen."

"Sure." She leans toward me, and I smile before kissing her lips.

She stops me when I start to pull away. She whispers, "Hold on," as her eyes drop to my mouth. She lifts her hand and slides her thumb across my lips, then smiles. "There." She shows me the lipstick on the edge of her thumb.

I want to drag her back against me and kiss her again and ruin her lipstick, but we don't have time. As soon as I get to the kitchen, Mouse jumps from his hiding spot on top of the cabinets. I barely catch him and rub the top of his head before setting him on the counter to give him a couple of treats.

Leah's heels click on the hardwood a moment later before she comes around the corner, smiling. "You're going to make him fat if you keep giving him so many treats."

"Should I tell you the same thing about Bruce?" Her nose scrunches in response, making me grin.

"Whatever," she states. "Are you ready?"

"Almost." I pick up the flowers she hasn't noticed, and her eyes light up.

"You got me flowers?"

"This wouldn't be a date if I didn't."

She smiles and takes them from me, then holds the soft pink petals to her nose. "Thank you. They're beautiful."

I kiss her forehead. "Glad you like them."

"I love them. I'll put them in a vase when we get home." She looks up at me. "We should go before someone shows up or you get a phone call and have to leave," she teases.

"Let's go before that happens." I laugh, which is something I do all the time now that I'm around her. I take the flowers from her and set them on the counter before leading her to the living room and helping her with her coat.

On the way to the restaurant, we talk, and like always, conversation comes easy. Really, everything with her is easy. She's not the kind of woman who plays games to get what she wants or the kind of woman who says what she thinks I want to hear. She's the opposite of the women I've dated in the past. She's just Leah—she tells it like it is, even when she's not completely comfortable with a certain topic.

"I love this place," she says excitedly, sitting forward in her seat when we reach the steak house. "They have the best pepper steak, and they serve it with this cheesy rice that I've never been able to replicate at home."

"Maybe you can ask for the recipe tonight?" I joke while parking.

She snorts. "I've tried that, but the chef is tight lipped. He said it's an old family recipe, and only his son will get it, when he's on his deathbed."

"Only you would actually try to get a recipe from the chef."

She shrugs. "It's delicious, and you'll understand why I want it when you taste it for yourself." She unhooks her belt as I get out and meet her at her car door. I take her hand. As soon as we walk into the restaurant, I give my name to the maître d', and we're escorted to our table. I help Leah with her coat and then into her seat before taking my own across from her. We order a bottle of house white from the maître d' just as our waiter shows up to introduce himself. While pouring our water, he tells us the dinner specials and lets us know that he'll be back after we've had time to look over our menus. Finally alone with Leah, I look across the table and notice her eyes focused on something across the room. I follow her gaze to a good-looking man and woman sitting a few tables away.

"Do you know them?" At my question her head flies my way, and she presses her lips together tightly. Reading her annoyed expression, I ask, "Who are they?"

"My ex . . ." She shakes her head. "Chris, the guy I told you about running into the other day."

I glance across the room at him quickly. "The guy who can't commit."

"Exactly," she mumbles, picking up her napkin and placing it on her lap with jerky movements.

Jealousy curls in the pit of my stomach, and I growl without thinking, "Do you still have feelings for him?"

At my question she laughs hard, tossing her head back, then looks me in the eye. "You can't be serious," she says, still laughing. "I feel only regret when it comes to him." She wipes under her eyes as she gets her laughter under control. "I just wish I had the courage to go over to their table and tell his new girlfriend exactly the kind of man she's sitting with."

My jealous feelings gone, I reach across the table and nab her hand. "I'd rather you not do that, at least not tonight," I say softly.

"I won't, even if I want to," she replies just as softly, looking into my eyes. "She might deserve a heads-up, but I'm not messing up our first date. Not even for the sisterhood."

Smiling, I bring her fingers to my lips and kiss them. "Good. Though this is far from our first date, according to my calculations."

"True." Her fingers tighten around mine. "That said, we should probably check out the menu."

"I thought you were set on having the pepper steak?"

"I am, but you haven't figured out what you're having, and I still need to check out the appetizers. I'm starving and need something to snack on before dinner."

"Let me know what looks good, baby." I release her hand and watch her heated eyes roam over me. "I'm a sure thing, beautiful." I wink. "And you're gonna need energy for what I have planned for you tonight." I nod at the menu. "Figure out what you're having so we can eat and get to that part of our night." Without another word, she drops her eyes from mine with a smile on her lips and starts to look over the menu.

Not long after, our waiter comes back to drop off a basket of warm bread and take our orders. Leah tells him that we'd like the shrimp cocktail before dinner, and I order a beer, because regardless of how great the maître d' made the wine sound, I know I won't enjoy it.

After the waiter walks away and we're served wine, Leah leans toward me. "Are you excited about seeing your parents?"

I start to tell her how things might go when she meets my parents—especially my mother—but stop when a shadow falls over our table. I look up to see who's joined us, and my hackles rise.

"Leah." Her name leaving her ex's mouth sets my teeth on edge, and I fight back a curse. I swear, if he says anything to ruin our night, I'm going to lose my mind.

"Chris," Leah replies, and there's no missing the edge of annoyance in her tone. The woman at Chris's side nervously looks between Leah and me and moves to stand slightly behind her man.

"Sorry for interrupting your evening," Chris says, looking at me uncertainly before focusing on Leah. "I just wanted to come over and introduce you to my fiancée, Darcy."

"What?" Leah looks at the woman hiding behind him.

"After our conversation, I thought about what you said, and, well, you were right. Thank you."

"What conversation?" Darcy asks, looking up at Chris and frowning slightly.

"I'll explain it later, honey." He gently looks down at her with a soft expression.

Leah looks stunned by this news. I grab her hand and attention, and she looks at me for a moment before shaking her head. "Um, that's great. Congratulations, you two."

"Thank you." Chris nods, then places his arm around Darcy's shoulders. "We'll let you get back to dinner—have a nice evening." He walks off without another word, and I wonder if maybe Leah laying into him woke him up. I hope it did, for his sake and his fiancée's.

"Well, that was odd," Leah mutters, bringing my attention to her. She shakes her head slowly, then mumbles, "Did you see how he looked at her?"

"I saw."

She nods and studies me, then smiles brightly before grabbing a piece of bread and swiping it through the butter in a ceramic dish. "I think he loves her. I really do hope that things work out for them."

I'm not surprised by her statement; she seems to want everyone to be happy, however that happiness comes about.

"Maybe you'll get an invitation to the wedding," I joke, and the sound of her laughter makes my chest feel warm and light.

"If I do, you're coming as my plus-one," she says sassily, and I smile just as the waiter appears with the shrimp cocktail and my beer. I take a drink while Leah picks up one of the shrimp, dunks it in the cocktail sauce, takes a bite, and groans. "You have to have one—they're awesome," she instructs me after she chews and swallows. I grab one and follow her lead.

She's right, they are awesome, but not as awesome as my prime rib or her pepper steak and cheesy rice, which is so delicious I'm tempted to ask the chef for the recipe myself. After we finish our meals, we order a slice of chocolate fudge cake to go, and I pay before leading Leah back out of the restaurant.

"Drunk?" I ask her as I lift her into my truck.

"No," she lies. Her eyes are glassy, and she has a silly smile on her face. She drank almost the entire bottle of wine by herself, because I could only stomach a sip.

"Don't pass out on me. You have cake to eat, and I'm curious about what you've got on under this dress." I run my hand across her stomach as I buckle her in.

"I'm not going to pass out," she replies breathlessly.

"Good." I lean in and kiss her because I can't help myself and pull away only when her fingers tighten in my hair and she moans against my tongue. I feel her heated stare as I shut her door and head around to the driver's side. When I get in, I start the engine and back out of the parking space.

Her hand lands on my thigh, and I grab it and lace our fingers together. "Thank you for dinner. Tonight was perfect—a perfect first date," she says.

"Anytime, baby." I give her fingers a squeeze. I might have to disagree with her about it being the perfect first date. I'll never forget waking her up after a fucked-up night, only to find she'd made it her mission to rectify the evening by setting her kitchen table and serving up Chinese food by candlelight. "It was a good night."

"The best." She leans over and rests her head against my shoulder.

As I drive us home, her weight settles against me, and I know she's fallen asleep. After I park in her driveway, I carry her up the walk and manage to get her inside. I place her in bed and smile when her lashes don't even flutter, and I pull the quilt over her. I take Bruce out, and when I get back inside, I give Mouse a couple more treats before going back to the bedroom, where Leah is still passed out. I take off her shoes, dress, and lacy bra and leave her in her lace panties. As disappointed as I am, I have to admit she's adorable, even though she's passed out. After I remove my own clothes, I get into bed and tuck her against my chest and wrap my hand around her hip. I listen to her breathing and fall asleep with her right where she belongs.

"Why did I drink so much?" Leah groans as she rolls away from me, dragging me out of sleep.

I roll with her and rest my hand lightly on her stomach. "Sick?"

"Headache," she mumbles. She lifts her hands to her face and covers her eyes. "Remind me to never drink again."

"I'll stop you next time." I smile and kiss the side of her head. "What time do you need to be at work?"

"Eleven." She sighs, peeking at me between her fingers. I glance at the clock. It's just after nine.

"You have time to shower and eat. I'll start the water, make you breakfast, and feed Mouse before I take Bruce with me. I need to take him home since he doesn't have food here, but I'll be back after that."

Her eyes close; then she says suddenly, "I passed out on you last night."

"What?"

She looks at me. "I fell asleep on the way home last night. And obviously you put me to bed."

"Yeah," I agree, confused by where she's going with this.

"Sometimes I'm sure that you can't possibly be real; you're too good to be true. I love you."

"I love you too."

She bites her lip, and her cheeks suddenly darken.

"I didn't . . . we didn't—"

I grin, cutting her off. "You can make it up to me tonight." I kiss her bare shoulder. "Right now, just focus on getting in the shower and feeling better."

"Maybe you should shower with me."

I fight back laughter. "Baby, if I shower with you, you're—"

She cuts me off. "I figure you'll make me feel better." She rolls toward me, her soft breasts pressing into my chest. Her hands slowly slide up my waist as she lowers her face to kiss me above my heart. "Please."

There's no way I'll be able to deny her, so I pull her up against me and roll us out of bed. I stand and look down into her beautiful face. "All right, temptress, we'll shower; then I'll make you breakfast after I take Bruce home."

Her smile is smug, and I ignore it as I lead her to the bathroom. I flip on the shower and turn toward her. Seeing her standing in nothing but a pair of deep-blue lace panties, her hair in messy waves down around her shoulders, I can't believe she's mine. I move toward her and place both my hands on her hips. With my thumbs in the lace, I slide the fabric down until it drops and pools at her ankles. "Step out, baby," I say, which she does one foot at a time before kicking the light fabric away. Her hands come up to rest against my chest, and I remove my boxers. My cock springs free, and her heated gaze drops to it as she wraps her hand around it. Her hand slides up and then back down, and I growl, wrapping my hand around hers to stop her. "In the shower, now."

Her eyes meet mine, and she nods before she follows me in under the warm spray.

I pull away from her tight grasp, then drop to my knees and look into her eyes before burying my face between her legs, lapping, sucking, and devouring her until she comes on my tongue and fingers, her moans amplified in the quiet space. My cock is throbbing as I stand, and I'm caught off guard when she drops to her knees and takes my full length between her lips. I rest both hands against the shower wall while I watch myself disappear as her hand works, twisting and jerking on each and every downward stroke. "Fuck, baby." I touch her face. When her eyes meet mine, I warn her, "Gonna come." She doesn't back off at my warning. She sucks harder and takes me deeper while locking her nails into the back of my thigh, holding me close. I roar, my hips jerking, my mind blanking of anything and everything but her and me. I look down into her eyes and groan when she releases me from her mouth and kisses the tip of my cock. I pull her up and against me and kiss her hard, thrusting my tongue between her parted lips. The kiss seems to last forever, taking and giving everything both of us need. When we finally drag our mouths away, we're both breathing heavy, and we look into each other's eyes. I rest my forehead to hers and cup her jaw. "Never, never thought I'd find this, feel this." I grab her hand and bring it up to rest over my wildly beating heart. "I love you, Leah. With every part of me, I love you."

She drops her forehead to my chest while wrapping her arms around my waist. "I love you, Tyler, more than I ever thought it was possible to love another person." Hearing that, I know without a doubt that whatever we face, whatever happens, nothing else will ever matter, as long as we keep hold of each other.

Suggestion 12

STAY POSITIVE

LEAH

This was a bad idea.

I knew it was a bad idea when Tyler asked me to come home with him for Thanksgiving after we'd known each other for such a short time. I knew it was an even worse idea after Heather warned me about their mom, but sitting in Tyler's parents' living room, I know this was the stupidest idea in the history of ideas.

His parents hate me. Okay, maybe his dad doesn't hate me, but his mom for sure does. She's been nice enough, but every time she gets a chance to bring up one of Tyler's exes or a woman he once knew, she's done it without pause. I know Tyler can tell I'm more than a little uncomfortable. He's tried to comfort me; he hasn't let go of my hand and is constantly giving me reassuring looks.

I'm not sure it will be okay. She hasn't let up, even after he's repeatedly told her to stop. The only silver lining is that we're not staying with his parents while we're in town. Lucky for me, Tyler rented a small cabin for us in the middle of the woods for the few days we're here. I don't think I could handle his mom for more than a few hours at a time.

Actually, I know I couldn't without a ton of alcohol and a few therapy sessions afterward.

"Nicole asked about you," his mom says, sparing me a quick glance before continuing. "I told her you were coming for Thanksgiving, and she said she'd stop by."

"What the fuck?" Tyler growls.

"Patty," his father says in a warning tone even I recognize.

"You two were friends before you were a couple, and then even after you broke up. I don't know what the big deal is," Patty says, running her hands down the front of her dress slacks as she takes a seat on the couch next to Tyler. She's really pretty, with an oval face, brown eyes that are striking against her light complexion, and shoulder-length brown hair that is tied back in a bun. Tyler's father looks like an older version of him, from his hair to his eyes. He's still handsome at his age.

"We're leaving." Tyler gets up, pulling me with him to stand. "I'll see you both on Thanksgiving, but just a warning." He glares at his mom and glances at his dad. "If anyone besides family is here when we arrive tomorrow, that's the last you'll see of me for a long fucking while."

"Son." His dad stands from his recliner, but Tyler ignores him while dragging me toward the door. He stops as we reach it and locks eyes with his mom, who looks somewhat worried now.

"FYI, Mom, I love this woman. I'm going to marry her one day and eventually have babies with her. It would really fucking suck if they lived their lives not knowing their grandmother because she can't seem to grow the fuck up."

"Tyler!" his dad barks.

"No, Dad, even you gotta know this shit is whacked." He shakes his head, then pulls me out the front door, leaving it wide open as he drags me to his truck and places me inside. I buckle in while he gets behind the wheel. I don't want to look, but my eyes lift, and I see his mom standing in the open front door with what look like tears in her eyes. I watch his dad wrap his arms around her and pull her inside, shutting the door.

"I'm sorry, baby." Tyler scrubs his hands down his face. "Fuck, I thought . . . I thought she would lay off after she met you and saw how happy I am."

"It's okay," I try to reassure him, and his angry eyes come to me.

"It's not okay, Leah. None of that shit she said was okay."

"You're right, but then again, it could've been worse."

"Worse?" He looks doubtful.

"Well . . ." I roll my lips together. "For starters, all of the women she mentioned could have been here to welcome you home." His lips twitch slightly. "She probably didn't invite them because there was no way all of them could fit in the living room."

"Why, when I'm so fucking pissed that I'm seeing red, do I still wanna laugh?"

I ignore his comment and add quietly, "You've dated a lot."

"Yeah," he agrees. He reaches over and grabs my hand while wrapping his other hand around the back of my neck to pull me closer. "Not one of them had the power to hold me, baby. Not one of them made me look forward to my future the way you do."

"You don't have to convince me. I know I couldn't feel what I do without you feeling the same in return," I say softly, and he leans forward, brushing his lips against mine.

"Any other woman I know would be running for the hills or pissed about what just happened and be demanding an explanation," he replies as he releases me to turn on his truck and then back out of his parents' driveway.

"Heather warned me this might happen," I admit as he drives down his parents' quiet street. Their neighborhood is beautiful. All the houses are a deep-red brick, but none are shaped exactly alike. There are full-grown trees everywhere that have changed with the season, and I imagine this would be a great place to grow up or to raise a family. Even the town is cute. It's not very big, but it's nestled within the Smoky Mountains and looks like something out of a picture book.

"What?" Tyler asks, pulling me back into the conversation.

"Heather said your mom didn't want you to move and has been trying to convince you to come back to town since you left. She said she might play dirty."

I bite the inside of my cheek when he growls, "And you still came with me?"

I defend myself. "You wanted me to come. How would you have felt if I bailed on you?"

"I'd be pissed."

"Exactly." I roll my eyes. "Plus, I know you love your mom, and so does Heather, so I convinced myself she couldn't be *that* bad."

"What are you thinking now that you've met her?" he asks, sounding somewhat sarcastic.

"I think she misses her son and is desperate to have him home," I tell him, reaching over to rest my hand on top of his.

I watch him pull in a deep breath and let it out. "It's not even about me," he says, and I start to frown. "She didn't want Heather to move to Montana after she met Marvin and he asked her to live with him there. She got over it somewhat when Heather and he got married, but when things between them started to go downhill after Heather had Kennedy, she hated that she wasn't just a short drive away from her daughter."

"That's understandable," I point out. My mom would probably act the same in the same circumstance.

"It is, but it isn't. I moved because I found a better opportunity for myself, not because I found a woman. Yes, I met you right after I moved, but even if I hadn't met you, I still would not be moving home. I like where I am. I like the town. I like the people. And now, with you there, I know it's where I'm going to stay. My mom is going to have to get over it. We live less than six hours apart. I'm not in China."

I smile. He's right. The drive actually flew by a lot more quickly than I thought.

"Just give her time. Hopefully, she'll see you're happy and find a way to deal with how she feels about you being gone."

"As optimistic as you are, I'm tempted to go to the store, get shit for Thanksgiving, and spend tomorrow locked away with you in the cabin."

"As wonderful as that idea sounds, and it does sound *really* wonderful, I don't think that would be wise," I say as he pulls up in front of our home away from home for the time we're here. "I saw her crying at the door before your dad forced her inside. She's upset. She loves you. Maybe you got through to her." He looks doubtful. "And maybe you didn't." I squeeze his hand. "But I'm not going to let her scare me off, if that's what you're afraid of."

"And if someone from my past shows up at their house tomorrow?" he asks worriedly, looking at me.

"I'll thank them for not being able to keep you." I smile. "Unless they come on to you or touch you. Then all bets are off, because you're mine."

He grins. "Possessive?"

"Yes." I'm not even ashamed.

Before I know what's happening, my seat belt is unhooked and he's dragging me over the center console and onto his lap. "Are you mine, then?"

"You know I am," I say breathlessly as he slides his hand up my outer thigh, under my shirt, and over my waist and then stops with his thumb curved under my lace-covered breast.

"I think I might need you to prove it."

"How would you like me to do that?" I moan when his thumb slides up and across my nipple.

"I'll explain the ways in detail as soon as I get you inside."

"Are you going to kiss me before then?" I drop my eyes to his mouth, which is so close I can feel each and every one of his breaths.

"Hell yeah." He smiles, but what he doesn't do is kiss me.

I shift on his lap, feeling his erection under me, and my core tightens in anticipation. "Tyler, you really need to kiss me."

"Mmm." His thumb sweeps across my nipple again, catching on the lace, and my back arches.

"Tyler," I warn.

"Can't I look at you for a minute?"

"No," I deny with a shake of my head as my fingers shift and dig into his hard shoulders.

"All right, baby, I'll kiss you." He slides his nose across mine, then kisses my earlobe, asking there, "Better?"

"No." My voice is raspy as he nips it with his teeth, sending a shock wave right to my core.

"Here?" He kisses down my neck over my pulse, which is beating rapidly.

"No."

"Where do you want me to kiss you, Leah?" I start to open my mouth to tell him on the lips but whimper when his hand slides down and cups me between my legs. "Do you want me to kiss you here?"

God, yes. My eyes slide closed. "That would be okay."

"The problem is, baby, I don't just want to kiss you here." His fingers dig in. "I want to eat you until you're screaming my name. Then I want to tongue fuck your tight, hot, sweet, wet pussy until you beg me to stop."

"Holy cow."

"You ready for that?"

Since I can't speak, I nod, and when I do, he captures my mouth in a deep kiss. The kiss isn't like any we've ever shared before. It's earth shattering, branding, and a lead-up to what's to come. Still kissing me, he somehow gets his door open and me out with him. I wrap my legs around his hips, and he carries me up to the porch and inside. When the door closes behind us, my back hits the wall in the entryway, and he uses his hips to hold me up as he removes my top and then my bra in one swift movement. I work on the buttons of his flannel, wanting to feel his skin against mine, but before I get very far, he tears his mouth from mine and puts me down. When my feet hit the floor, he stands back.

"Kick off your shoes."

I do as he unhooks the button of my jeans and slides them and my panties down over my hips and knees. I kick both pieces of clothing to the side as his fingers trail along my stomach. I whimper when he drops to his knees, closing his mouth over my sex and dragging his tongue back and forth over my clit. My head falls back, and my clit pulses.

"Tyler." I gasp for breath as he captures my hips with both his big hands, pulling me closer to his mouth. "Oh God." I force my eyes to open and look down at the top of his head. Letting out a loud cry, I slide my fingers into his thick hair and roll my hips against his mouth. As I come, my head falls back against the wall with a thud, and my body starts to go limp.

"We're not even close to done," he tells me, locking one hand around my hip to keep me upright while sliding two fingers through my wet folds, circling my clit, then my entrance. My hips jerk in response, and our eyes lock. "You're so wet." He slips the tip of one finger inside me, swirling it. "So fucking wet." My breathing is labored as he slides his finger out and replaces it with two, rubbing them up against my G-spot. "Put your leg over my shoulder, baby. Offer me up what belongs to me."

I don't hesitate. I lift my leg up over his shoulder, using my hands still in his hair for balance. As I'm spread open for him, his eyes drop from mine to between my legs, and he leans forward, circling my clit with his tongue. He groans against me as his fingers move ruthlessly inside me. My fingers hold tight to his hair as I cry out, feeling the muscles of my lower belly pulling tight.

"Tyler!" My hips jerk erratically as I slide over the edge again, seeing blinding white light on the outer edges of my vision. As I'm coming down from the high he just gave me, he picks me up, and I force my muscles to work as I lock my legs around his hips and my arms around his shoulders. I hear his boots hitting the stairs and know we're heading up to the loft bedroom. I lick his neck and kiss his ear, then nibble my way along his jaw to his mouth.

"Fuck, baby." He stops on the stairs, kissing me back as I fumble with his shirt. I let out a moan when I finally get it off his shoulders, and my breasts press against his warm skin. He groans in response, lifting me higher in his arms before he starts to move us up the stairs once more. When we hit the loft, he drops me to my back on the bed and looks down at me with his chest heaving. He bends, takes off his boots, then shrugs his shirt the rest of the way off. Him in nothing but his jeans, his hair a mess from my fingers, and his eyes dark with desire—I don't think I've ever been more turned on by the sight of him, even after coming twice already.

He unsnaps the buttons of his jeans and drags them down over his hips. His erection springs free, bouncing against his stomach, and my pulse quickens. He puts one knee on the bed and then the other while wrapping his hand around his length, and I spread my legs for him. He slides the tip up and down through my folds before he slides deep in one long stroke.

"Yes." I hold on to his waist and lift my thighs, pressing them into his sides as he slides out, then back in. "Harder," I beg, lifting my mouth to his. "Fuck me harder."

With a growl, he gives me what I want and moves his hips harder and faster. I press my head back into the pillow and swivel my hips with each and every stroke.

"Tyler." I know it's coming. I feel the pull in my belly and know it's not going to take much more to send me over the edge.

"Not yet." He sits back, then rolls, and I settle on top of him with his hard cock still buried deep and his big hands on my ass. "Ride me," he orders, thrusting his hips up into mine. "Hard and fast, baby."

I lower my mouth to his as I lift my hips, then fall down on his length. The sound of our flesh meeting fills the air, along with our heavy breathing. Wrapping his hand in my hair, he arches me away from him and leans up, capturing one of my breasts in his hot mouth. I moan, and my hips buck hard against his as he moves from one breast to the other while holding me in place, keeping me where he wants me.

"Tyler, please." I grab hold of his shoulders as he tugs hard on my nipple, sending a bolt of electric shock right to my clit. He lets go of my hair, then releases my nipple, taking my hips in both his hands. He lifts me up and slams me down over and over, so hard my breath catches. My name leaves his mouth on a loud roar, and my pussy ripples as I orgasm hard, feeling him come deep inside me. I fall against his chest, and his arms wrap around me, his chin settling in the crook of my neck.

We stay like that for a long time, our skin damp, our hearts pounding, our breathing labored. Only when I shiver does he move. He lies back with me still against his chest and pulls the blanket from the end of the bed up over my back. "I love you," he says.

"I love you too." I tip my head back to see his face.

"How about we shower? Then I want to take you into town to one of my favorite restaurants for dinner."

"Is it a dress-up kind of restaurant?" I question, not really in the mood to move, much less get dressed up to go out to dinner.

"Nope." He smiles. "You'll like it. They've got nothing but hamburgers, fries, and beer on the menu. And the burgers are better than anything else you've ever eaten."

"You know the way to my heart." I smile, pulling my hand from the blanket so I can touch his jaw. Running my fingers along the slight scruff, I say softly, "I should call Grams and Noah to check on Mouse and Bruce."

"It was cool of Noah to keep him for me."

"He likes you, and the boys love Bruce. It's not a big deal," I reply.

He rolls me to my back, sliding out of me, and then covers my mouth with his before pulling back. "You can call them after we shower."

I'm unable to respond, because he covers my mouth once more.

Suggestion 13

BE A BADASS

LEAH

"Thanks again for looking after Bruce, and tell the boys and Angie I love them," I say to my brother Noah as I stand in front of the bathroom mirror in nothing but one of Tyler's flannel shirts I haphazardly buttoned up and my panties.

"I will. Love you, sis. Have fun."

"Love you too." I hang up with him as Tyler comes out of the shower, wrapping a towel around his waist.

"Everything okay with Bruce?" he asks, coming to stand at the sink next to me and loading a toothbrush with paste.

"Noah said Bruce is doing great and that even Angie, who's never really wanted a dog, adores him and is now begging him to get a puppy for the boys for Christmas." He grins at that. "So I guess the boys will be getting a puppy."

"He loves his wife and his boys, so that'd be my guess too."

"Yeah." I look away from him so I can dial Grams. I put the call on speaker and listen to it ring while I dig out my mascara from my makeup bag.

"Sugar." I hear the smile in Grams's voice. "Your mom and I were just talking about you. How'd things go with Tyler's family?" she asks, and I pause with my mascara wand an inch from my lashes. I glance at Tyler, who's still standing next to me in nothing but a towel, brushing his teeth and listening to the conversation.

"It went great," I lie, watching Tyler shake his head. I shrug and mouth, *What?*

"I'm happy to hear that, sugar. I know you were nervous about meeting them. I told you everything would be okay."

Feeling a little guilty for lying, I ask, "Is Mouse doing okay?" as I swipe on mascara, then look through my bag again for my bronzer.

"I don't know," she mumbles, sounding distracted, and my heart sinks.

"You don't know?"

"He's been hiding since you dropped him off. The only reason I know he's alive is the food and treats I leave out are disappearing."

"He'll come out eventually. Just be prepared for him to scare the crap out of you when he does."

"I'll remember that," she assures me, and then I hear my mom talking in the background. "Your mom wants to talk to you before she heads home."

"Okay, love you."

"Love you too. See you when you get home in a couple days."

"See you then, and have a good Thanksgiving."

"You too, sugar." Grams passes the phone to Mom.

"Hey, honey, how was the drive? Is everything going okay? Do you like Tyler's parents? Are you having fun?"

I smile at her barrage of questions, then answer. "It's going good. Tyler rented us a beautiful cabin not far from his parents' house. But you should see the town, Mom. It's like something out of a picture book."

"Text me some photos when you can," she orders, then softens her voice. "I can't wait to hear all about your trip when you get home. We're going to miss you and Tyler at dinner tomorrow."

"We'll be home Sunday afternoon. If we're early enough, we'll come to dinner."

"Okay, honey. Tell Tyler's parents I said hi, and don't forget to check in. I want to know how things are going."

"I will," I agree as I finish applying bronzer while Tyler leaves the bathroom. "Love you. Tell Dad I love him and everyone else hi."

"Will do. Love you, and we'll talk soon."

"Talk soon." I hang up and place my cell on the counter just as Tyler comes back into the bathroom shirtless, wearing his jeans zipped up but not buttoned.

"You didn't tell your grandma or mom about what happened," he states, stepping up behind me and wrapping an arm around my waist.

I meet his gaze in the mirror as I add some blush. "I don't want them to worry about me, and if I tell them what happened, they will. Plus, if our families meet one day, I don't want this clouding my family's opinion of your mom."

"Baby—"

"I'm hoping that I can win your mom over while we're here and that this will be something we all laugh about later on."

"I get that, but I want you to know you can be honest. I don't want you to feel like you can't talk to them about it."

"I'm just keeping things to myself for right now." I rest my hand over his on my stomach when it growls. "How far is the restaurant? I'm starving."

"I hear that." He smiles. "Not far, about fifteen minutes. How much longer till you're ready?"

"I'm ready now," I say, watching his eyes rake over me in his shirt, which doesn't hide much of anything. "I just need to get dressed." I turn in his arms and place my hands against his chest when he slides his hands down my back to cup both my ass cheeks. "I'm hungry."

"So am I." He starts to lower his mouth to mine, but I dodge his kiss and laugh.

"I need food." I push at his chest, not even gaining an inch. "Unfortunately, I don't think my body can survive on orgasms alone."

"Maybe we should see if it's possible, just for scientific purposes," he says while leading me out of the bathroom backward toward the bed. Unable to help myself, I lean up and kiss him, moaning into his mouth as he slides his hands under the lace covering my ass, grabbing two handfuls. My stomach growls even louder just as the backs of my knees hit the bed, and he tugs his mouth from mine. "We'll have to experiment another time," he concedes as I laugh. He lets me go and picks up his shirt from the bed, pulling it on over his head. "While you get dressed, I'm going to call my dad back. He hasn't stopped calling since we left the house."

"Sure." I give him what I hope is a reassuring smile, but I'm sure it looks more like a grimace.

"I'll meet you downstairs when you're ready." He picks up his boots and kisses me once more before heading down the steps and leaving the loft.

I put the jeans I had on earlier back on, then dig through my bag to find a bra and a sweater. After I put both on, I go to the bathroom and brush out my hair. Once I'm done, I go downstairs and get on my shoes, which are near the front door, then search for Tyler. I find him in the kitchen, leaning against the counter with a hand wrapped around the back of his neck, the other holding his cell to his ear.

Not wanting to interrupt, I give him some privacy and walk through the cabin and out the sliding glass door off the living room. I lean against the banister at the edge of the deck and breathe in the crisp fall air. The view is amazing. There are nothing but treetops and twinkling lights as far as the eye can see. I love the beach; it's one of my favorite places in the world. But I could definitely get used to being surrounded by the forest.

The sliding glass door opens behind me, and Tyler comes out. Judging by the look on his face, the phone call wasn't a good one. "Is everything okay?"

"Dad's pissed at me for the way I spoke to Mom. He wants me to apologize to her." I bite the inside of my cheek. He was harsh with his mom, but I understand why he was. I hope his mom and dad do too. He comes closer, fitting his front to my back. "He also said that no one but family will be at the house tomorrow. That I shouldn't worry about that, and neither should you."

"That's good, right?" I ask, feeling that his muscles are still tight with tension.

"Yeah, except he didn't say anything about Mom being sorry for the way she acted toward you, so I'm not sure what we'll be walking into tomorrow." He sighs, and I turn around to face him, holding on to his waist.

"Whatever happens, it will be okay."

He closes his eyes and drops his forehead to mine. "I won't put up with anyone disrespecting you, Leah, and that includes my mom."

I give his waist a squeeze and wait until he looks at me. "Let's not think about that right now. Let's just see how things go tomorrow."

"Are you always so optimistic?" he asks, pulling his forehead away from mine and curving his hand around my jaw. He runs his thumb across my chin and the edge of my bottom lip.

My nose scrunches. "No . . . or I haven't been before." I give a slight shrug. "With you, things are different. I don't want to think about the bad stuff that might or might not happen; I just want to be with you and enjoy each moment we have together." I rest the side of my head against his chest and slide my hands around his waist, holding on to him tightly. "I have to believe things will work out and that your mom will come around. Not for me, but for you, because you deserve that from her."

I feel his lips at the top of my head, then listen to him whisper, "Fuck, I love you." I tip my head back and kiss his jaw. "Let's go eat."

"Finally," I sigh dramatically. "I thought I'd have to beg you to feed me."

He chuckles, and we go into the house. After helping me with my coat, he gets his on; then we get in his truck. The drive into town takes about fifteen minutes longer than it should, because I point out a street to Tyler that's already lit with Christmas lights, and Tyler turns in so we can take in all the houses and decorations.

When we finally reach the center of town, Tyler parks in one of the empty lots. He explains that we'll have to walk, because there will be no parking where we're going. After we both get out, he takes my hand in his and leads me down a busy sidewalk packed with people. I'm surprised by the number of people out and about, shopping and eating at the local restaurants the night before Thanksgiving. My hometown is a ghost town the night before a big holiday, and the only place people seem to be is at the grocery store, getting last-minute supplies so they won't have to go to the store in the morning before it closes for the day.

"This place is amazing," I tell Tyler as we head down Main Street. The silver light poles every few feet are wrapped with red ribbon, making them look like candy canes, and each and every shop we pass has the windows painted with holiday scenes as Christmas carols are heard coming from overhead speakers.

"You like it?" Tyler looks down at me when we stop at a red light.

"It's magical." I glance around. "I feel like I'm on the set of a Hallmark Christmas movie."

He looks around, and I wonder what he's thinking. "I never thought of it like that before. I guess I got so used to it I didn't really see it for anything more than the town I grew up in."

"I get that." I squeeze his hand. "After living in Mount Pleasant for so long, I don't really think about the fact that one of the most beautiful beaches around is a stone's throw away from my house. I think we all tend to take things for granted when they're available to us anytime. For instance, I have a friend who lives in New York, and she's never been to see the Statue of Liberty. I tell her all the time she needs to go. People save their whole lives to vacation in New York just so they can see it, and it's just a cab and boat ride away for her."

"She's never gone?"

"Nope."

"Have you seen it?" he asks, studying me.

"Twice," I reply as we head across the street when the light turns green. "I went with my parents and brothers when I was about thirteen. We drove to New York and spent a weekend in the city. Besides sightseeing, Mom and I saw a couple shows, and the boys and Dad went to a baseball game." I look up at him. "I went again two years ago, when I took a master coloring class in Manhattan. While I was there, I did the whole tourist thing. It was only two days, but I saw every sight Manhattan has to offer, even if it was only from the top of one of the sightseeing buses."

"If you could go anywhere in the world, where would you go?" he asks, stopping and turning me toward him. He wraps a hand around my hip while peering down at me.

"Anywhere in the world?"

"Anywhere in the world." He nods, and I think about it for a moment.

There are a million places I want to see in the world, but only one of them really sticks out. "Rome," I blurt out, then shake my head. "I've always wanted to see the Colosseum and the Sistine Chapel, but I don't want to just go to Rome. I want to drink wine watching the sunset in Florence and walk the streets in Milan. I want to shop and eat until I can't eat any more, and then do it all again the next day."

"What about Egypt?" he asks.

"Egypt?"

"That would be my pick," he says with a small smile.

"Really?" I study him. "I never pegged you for the kind of guy who would be interested in going to Egypt."

"People are still trying to figure out how they were able to create some of the things they created. As a builder myself, the architecture fascinates me."

"I can see that." I smile, and he leans down, pressing his mouth against mine.

"Tyler." He turns his head, and I do the same. I watch a good-looking guy with a beanie on his head and a plaid shirt with a vest, jeans, and boots approach us on the sidewalk. "Shit, man! I thought that was you. What the fuck are you doing here?"

"Eli," Tyler says as he lets my waist go to accept a one-armed hug from him. "Good to see you, man."

"Please tell me you're moving back," Eli prompts with a hopeful look in his eyes.

Tyler glances down at me quickly before answering. "Sorry, man. I'm just in town for the holiday with Leah."

"Leah?" Eli finally notices me standing under Tyler's arm, and he blinks rapidly. "Shit, nice to meet you. Sorry. I . . . I didn't mean to interrupt. I just . . ."

"It's okay." I laugh. "Nice to meet you, Eli."

I hold out my hand, and he takes it. "You too." He looks from me to Tyler. "I see why you're not coming home."

"She's part of it, but you know the other part." Tyler tightens his hold on me.

"Yeah." Eli shoves his hands into his pockets. "Things haven't been the same since you left. Deck is an even bigger dick than he was before, and half of us are thinking about walking away. Putting up with his shit isn't worth the paycheck most of the time."

"Sorry to hear that, man," Tyler mutters, and Eli nods. "It's a long ways away, but if you ever think about moving, give me a call. I have a couple spots open, and I could use the help."

"Really?" Eli asks.

"For sure."

"Thanks," Eli says before he shakes his head. "I should let you go. I'm guessing you're here to eat." He nods to the side, and I look over and notice we're standing in front of a restaurant with dark-tinted windows that are painted with large Christmas wreaths made up of hamburgers.

"We are." Tyler nods.

Eli smiles. "Some of us are hanging out at Bark's down the block. You should stop by. I'm sure the guys would like to see you."

"We might do that."

"All right, have a good night, man." He looks at me. "It was nice meeting you, Leah."

"You too, Eli," I say.

He turns and starts to walk off down the sidewalk, but Tyler stops him by calling his name, and he turns his head our way. "My number hasn't changed. Call if you need to."

"Got it." Eli lifts his chin, and Tyler does the same before Eli disappears down the crowded sidewalk.

"They miss you," I state, and Tyler shrugs. "Do you miss working with them?"

"I miss the guys, but I don't miss the bullshit I had to put up with on a daily basis working for Deck," he explains.

I nod in understanding, then ask, "Do you miss it here?"

"Yes and no. Why?"

"Just curious if you'd want to move back here one day," I say, and his expression softens.

"I miss having my parents close and the friends I grew up with nearby, but I don't miss this town or my old job. I never wanted to live here forever, so when Scott offered me the job, I jumped on it. Don't get me wrong—this is a great town, but I want more for myself and any kids we have. There aren't a lot of opportunities here. Most of the people I grew up with moved away as soon as they had the chance to."

"It's a beautiful place to grow up," I tell him.

"It is," he agrees. "But so is Mount Pleasant."

"You're right, but just so you know, if you wanted to move back here, I would be okay with that. I think I would follow you anywhere."

"Do not say shit like that," he growls, and my heart sinks, startled by his demand.

"Wh-what?"

"Do not say shit like that when we're not alone or near a bed, where I can show you exactly what your words mean to me, baby. I swear to God, every fucking day, you prove to me exactly why life led you right through my window." A thrill skims down my spine. "Never—fucking never—did I think I would find a woman like you, a woman who makes me so fucking happy I have to question if she's fucking real. You, Leah, should not exist."

"Tyler—"

"Seriously, baby, you're understanding, accepting, and so damn beautiful that I look at you and can't believe you're mine."

"If you don't stop, I'm going to cry on the sidewalk in the middle of the perfect Hallmark movie town," I tell him, swallowing down tears.

"Don't cry, baby. Just know I appreciate what I have, know what it's worth, and will do everything within my power to keep it."

Tears I can't control fill my eyes, and when one falls, he catches it with his thumb, sweeping it away before touching his mouth to mine in a gentle kiss.

"No more tears," he says, swiping one off my other cheek.

I pull in a shaky breath. "It's your fault I'm crying."

"I know." He takes hold of my face. "But the longer you cry, the longer it's going to take me to feed you."

I shake my head. "I'm not normally emotional. I'm just crying because I'm starving."

"Right." He grins. "Are you done now?"

"I think so," I reply, and he kisses my forehead, then wraps his hand around mine and leads me across the sidewalk into the restaurant. The sign in the front says to seat ourselves, so we get a booth in the back and take off our coats; then we both sit on one side of the booth. "What do you recommend?" I ask. I pick up the menu and look it over.

"My favorite burger is called the Boom," he tells me, and I find that burger on the menu. It's two patties, cheese, bacon, and an over easy egg on toast.

"I'm not sure I'd enjoy having an egg on my hamburger."

"You can have a bite of mine," he assures me as the waitress comes over to take our drink orders. We both order beer, and when she comes back to drop them off, we place our dinner orders. I stick with my all-time favorite: a mushroom, swiss, and mayo, with a side of seasoned fries and ranch dressing to dip them in. Tyler orders his weird egg burger and regular fries.

About fifteen minutes later, she comes back to the table with two red trays overflowing with fries and burgers. "Enjoy, and let me know if you need anything else," she says.

I say thanks before she walks off, then look up at Tyler.

"Get ready, baby. After you take a bite from that, you're gonna be ruined," he warns me, and I pick up my hamburger, which is half-wrapped in white paper, and smile at him before I bring it to my mouth. My teeth sink into the soft bun and juicy meat, and the flavor hits my taste buds, making me groan. "Told you." He picks up his own burger and takes a bite.

I chew and swallow, then grab a fry and dunk it in ranch before popping it into my mouth. Holy cow, even the fries are better than any I've ever eaten, and the ranch is obviously homemade, with what tastes like finely chopped green onion.

"I'm so moving here just for this place," I tell him as I dunk another fry in ranch.

"We can come back anytime you want." He leans over, giving me a swift kiss.

"How's yours?" I eye his burger.

He shakes his head. "Take a bite."

I do, and even though it's an odd combination, it's still really fricking good. After we finish eating, he pays, because apparently I'm not allowed when I'm out with him, and then we get up and leave.

"Wanna go get a beer?" he asks when we hit the sidewalk outside.

"Sure."

We walk hand in hand down the street, which has gotten a little less crowded, and head toward the bar at the end of the block. When we get inside, Tyler orders us each a beer from the bar, and once we have our drinks, he leads me through the crowded room. The moment people start to notice him, they smile and wave or stop to say hello. He introduces me to everyone as his girlfriend, and I can't help but feel a little giddy every time he says it.

After I'm stopped and introduced to two guys he went to school with, we make it to a table where five guys are sitting, drinking beer, and laughing. I spot Eli in the group, and when he notices us, he grins and stands. He shouts Tyler's name and brings attention to us. All the guys turn, and when they do, they smile and stand. Tyler doesn't release my hand as he lifts his chin and gives out back pats to the guys. One of them brings over two chairs, but before I can sit in my own seat, Tyler pulls me down to sit on his lap. His fingers skim along the edge of my jeans, and I relax against him and sip on my beer. I listen to him and his friends talk and share stories, and I answer questions when they're directed at me.

When my bladder urges me to get up, I look around for the restroom sign, spotting it near the bar. I turn to look down at Tyler. "I need to use the restroom. I'll be right back."

"Do you know where it is?" he asks, and I nod my head. "All right, come right back to me," he orders, and I roll my eyes.

I get up and head toward a sign that directs me down a long hall. I notice a guy and a girl talking in the dim light at the end of the hall, but I don't pay much attention to them as I go into the single bathroom. After I take care of business, I wash my hands and leave the bathroom. I hear a hissed "Stop" and look back down the hall to where the man and woman were, and I notice the guy has the girl pressed to the wall.

For a moment, I think they're in the middle of a hot and heavy make-out session, but then I see the expression on her face and notice that her head is turned to the side, her eyes are closed, and her hands are pushing against his chest like she's trying to shove him off. Without thinking, I walk toward them and ask, "Is everything okay?"

The woman's eyes open to meet mine, and the guy growls, "Fuck off."

"Are you okay?" I ignore him, directing my question at her, and she gives a short sideways jerk of her head.

"Fuck off," the guy repeats, and I look at him.

"Let her go," I demand. His hold on her tightens, and pain fills her eyes.

"I said fuck off."

"I'm only going to ask you one more time." I get closer, and his eyes rake over me, his expression going from pissed to something else, something that makes me feel dirty.

"Yeah? What are you gonna do to me, gorgeous?"

"Break your nose." I shrug. "Maybe a finger or two."

He laughs, lets the girl go, and takes a step toward me. "So you think you can hurt me?" he asks as the girl sags against the wall before standing and rushing past me. I don't take my eyes off the guy coming toward me slowly, but I still wonder what the hell happened to girl code and woman power.

"I think I can kick your ass," I state, and he stops a few feet away. Even though he's bigger than I am, I'm not as afraid as I probably should be. My brothers and I used to fight all the time, but as I got older, they stopped fighting with me and started showing me how to defend myself against someone bigger and stronger.

"Give it your best shot, babe." He lunges at me, and I don't think. I ball my hand into a fist, pull my arm back, and swing. I feel the crack of cartilage under my knuckles and listen to him cry out in pain. He covers his nose with his hand as blood pours between his fingers. "You bitch!" he roars, rushing at me again.

Before he makes it to me, I'm picked up off the ground by arms that wrap around my waist. My legs flail, and I start to scream.

"Calm," Tyler orders against my ear as the broken-nose guy is tackled to the ground by two of Tyler's friends. He attempts to fight them off, but it's pointless. They're both bigger than he is.

My muscles relax, and I sag back into Tyler, listening to the guy on the floor complain about me breaking his nose. "Cops are on the way, Ty," someone says, and Tyler turns us to face the end of the hall, not letting up on the hold he has around me. "You good?"

"Yeah, but get me some ice for her hand."

"Got it." The guy grins at me, shaking his head before disappearing from sight.

Tyler half walks, half carries me to the women's bathroom, opens the door, and takes us in. He releases me when the door is closed, then turns to face me. "What the fuck were you thinking?" he roars as I shake out the hand I now notice is throbbing.

I take a step back from his fury but narrow my eyes. "He had a girl pinned to the wall. She didn't want to be pinned to the wall. He wouldn't let her go. What did you expect me to do?"

"I don't know, Leah. Maybe fucking come get your man to take care of shit."

"Why?" I frown. I go to the sink, turn on the cold water, and run it over my hand.

"*Why?*" he barks behind me, and I look up to see him glaring at my reflection in the mirror.

"Who knows what could have happened if I left him with her, Tyler? I wasn't going to do that, not when I could help her."

"You weigh maybe"—he jerks his chin up—"*maybe* a hundred and forty pounds, baby. That guy could have crushed you. He could've had a knife or a gun. What the fuck were you thinking, taking him on?"

"I was being a good person." I lift my chin. I will not feel guilty for what I did. I don't care if he's pissed or not. There's no way I would ever stand by and let a man or woman be harassed without stepping in.

"A good person?"

"Yes, a good person." I shake my head. "You weren't there. You didn't see the look on that girl's face as that guy tried . . . tried to . . . I don't know what he was trying to do for sure. But I know she didn't want it done to her."

"Fuck." He sifts his fingers through his hair.

"I need to go make sure she's okay." I start to move for the door, but he blocks it, cutting me off.

"She's fine. She's with Eli." His breathing is heavy, and I can see the pulse in his neck and the twitch in his jaw. "Give me your hand." I don't want to, but I still place my hand in his when he holds his out toward me, palm up. "How bad does it hurt?"

Right now I'm still on an adrenaline high, so I can't tell him for certain, but it does hurt. "It's okay."

His angry eyes meet mine. "Stop saying it's okay. It's not fucking okay."

"Okay," I whisper, and his jaw twitches. "Sorry, I mean it hurts a little, but ice will help."

Without another word, he pulls me from the bathroom and takes me to the front of the bar. Lifting me up, he plants me on a barstool, then accepts a bag of ice from the guy who was standing at the end of the hall earlier. Tyler holds the ice to my knuckles without a word or a look in my direction. I'm at a loss for what to say or do. I refuse to feel guilty for what I did, but I feel bad he's so upset.

Four cops arrive, and when they get to the bar, the man behind it takes them down the hall. When they reappear a few minutes later, two of the officers escort the guy with a bloody face out of the bar with his hands cuffed behind his back, and the man returns behind the bar.

"Drink this. It will help with the shakes," he says, and I swivel to face him as he places a glass of clear liquid in front of me.

"Thanks," I whisper, giving him a crooked smile while picking up the glass and taking a sniff. It smells like vodka, pure vodka. I take a sip and then another, allowing the liquid to calm my nerves.

"Since this rude fuck isn't gonna introduce me, I'll introduce myself. I'm Alan." Alan starts to reach for my hand, then shakes his head, pulling it back when Tyler grunts at him.

"Nice to meet you, Alan, and thanks for the drink." I hold it up.

"Anytime." He moves from behind the bar to stand next to Tyler when the two officers come over to talk to me. I tell them what happened, with Tyler standing over me, and the more I talk, the angrier I feel him get. I ignore him and give my statement, then watch them go talk to the girl across the room, who's been sitting with Eli. When the officers leave, she comes over to me.

"Are you okay?" I ask softly when she's close enough to hear me.

"Yes, thanks to you." Tears fill her eyes. "I . . . I told him to leave me alone, but . . . but he wouldn't let me go. I . . . I don't know what would have happened if . . ."

I notice that Eli, who's standing close to her, looks furious.

"I'm just glad you're okay," I murmur, cutting her off, and she wraps her arms around me, catching me off guard. When she lets me go, she looks up at Tyler. "I'm going home, but I'll see you tomorrow."

Wait, what? I look from her to Tyler and wonder what she's talking about. "See you tomorrow, Bell." He gives her a hug, and when he lets her go, she gives him a shaky smile.

"It was good seeing you, man," Eli says, looking at Tyler, and then his eyes come to me. "Thanks, Leah." He wraps an arm around Bell's shoulders and leads her away.

"You know her?" I ask Tyler, and he finally looks at me.

"She's my cousin. My mom's brother's stepdaughter."

"Oh." My stomach sinks. I thought his mom hated me before, but after she hears I got into a fight at a bar, she's really going to dislike me. This just keeps getting worse and worse. I pick up the glass of vodka and shoot the rest of it back. If I get drunk, it won't matter. Maybe I can stay drunk the rest of the weekend and pretend this has all been a bad dream.

When I feel a soft touch on my hand, I look at Tyler and notice his eyes are watching my hand as his fingers run over mine, inspecting my swollen knuckles. "I'm fine," I tell him softly. "It'll probably hurt for a couple days, but it's nothing I can't handle."

He doesn't respond. He looks behind the bar. "What do I owe you, man?"

"You're not paying," Alan says. "Drinks are on the house." His eyes move to me and then back to Tyler. "Now and always for you and your girl." He grins. "She's a badass. She deserves to drink for free."

"Shit," Tyler mutters. "Do not fucking encourage her."

"Not too many women would stand up to a guy like Dave, not when he's wasted. She did it, and she got Bell safe, giving him a bloody nose in the process. Sorry, bro, but your chick is a badass, and she should know it."

"She also could have gotten herself hurt, or worse."

"She's still right here listening to you talk about her like she's not," I point out, kind of drunk now. "I told you I'm okay."

"You tell me you're okay one more time, and I'm going to lose my goddamn mind and tan your hide, Leah." He glares at me.

"I'd like to see you try to spank me," I hiss, leaning toward him.

His eyes narrow, and he lowers his voice. "You're going to experience it, baby, so prepare."

He's not joking. I can tell by the look in his eyes. I narrow my eyes on his and hiss, "Try it." Then I look at Alan. "It was nice to meet you, and thank you for the vodka."

"Anytime." He grins at me, then claps Tyler on the shoulder. "Hopefully, I'll see you soon, man."

"Yeah." Tyler takes my hand and leads me out of the bar and down the sidewalk to his truck. He doesn't talk or reach for my hand as he drives us back to the cabin, and I can tell he's still pissed, which is beginning to piss *me* off. When we get inside, his phone rings, and he pulls it out of his pocket.

"Fuck, it's my dad. Go on up to bed. I'll be up in a bit," he says, not even looking at me.

I want to tell him to fuck off, but I don't. Instead, I stomp up the stairs, strip out of my clothes, put on a tee, and brush my teeth before I get into bed. I don't expect to fall asleep because I'm so annoyed, but somehow I end up passing out.

Suggestion 14

FIGHT IT OUT

LEAH

I lift my right hand to bring it up under my cheek, then groan when pain shoots through my fingertips. With the pain, memories of what happened last night at the bar flood my mind. I punched someone. Not just someone but a huge guy who deserved it but could have hurt me.

"Crap." I blink my eyes open and slowly sit up, looking at the place next to me in bed and then around the room. Tyler is nowhere in sight. I don't even know if he came to bed last night after his phone call with his dad. On that thought, worry starts to fill my stomach. I get up, go to the bathroom, and do my morning routine sluggishly, the pain in my hand slowing me down.

After I'm done, I start down the stairs, calling out to Tyler. I frown when he doesn't respond, and I go in search of him. He's not in the living room or the kitchen; he's not even outside on the back deck. When I go to the front door and look out the glass window, I see that his truck is gone.

"He left," I say to the empty room as the unease that's settled in my stomach grows, and my heart actually aches. I knew he was mad at me, but I didn't think he was mad enough to leave me here without a word. Feeling like I might cry, I go to the kitchen. I need to get my phone so I can call him and some caffeine to help me think and come up with a plan.

If he's so mad that he's not coming back, I need to go home. I know if I called my mom or my brothers, they'd come get me without a question. I also know that I can get a cab to the airport and book a flight once I'm there. I'm not crazy about the idea of waiting at the airport for hours and hours to catch a plane on Thanksgiving Day, but if I have to, I will. When I reach the kitchen, I find a small white piece of paper propped up against the coffeepot. I unfold it and close my eyes after I dissect Tyler's horrible penmanship.

Ran out to get you some pain meds. Be back soon.

He didn't leave me. He just went to the store. Relief hits me hard, and I lean against the counter. After a moment, I pour myself a cup of coffee and add milk and sugar, and then I start to go outside, needing some fresh air, but stop when someone knocks. When I turn to face the front door, my body gets tight. Tyler's mom is standing outside, and I can't even pretend like I'm not here, because she's looking directly at me through the window.

With a heavy sigh, I head to the door and unlatch the lock, opening it for her to come in. "Hey." I try to smile, but I know it looks as forced as it is. "Tyler isn't here. He went to the store."

"I know." She walks in, and her fancy boots click on the wood floor. I shut the door and pray she gets whatever she's going to say out quickly so I can drink my cup of coffee and figure out how to smooth things over with her son. "I heard about what happened last night." She turns to face me.

I cringe inwardly but lift my chin and stand a little taller. "Like I told Tyler, I won't apologize for what I did. I had to help. I couldn't just walk away."

She crosses her arms over her chest, scrutinizing me, and I realize that unlike her—dressed for the day in nice jeans and a sweater—I'm only wearing a T-shirt. I don't even have panties on. Talk about awkward.

"What you did was impulsive," she states.

"What do you think I should have done?" I ask, then shake my head and mutter, "Never mind." Even knowing it's rude, I hold up my hand, palm facing her. "I keep thinking about it, and I know if I had left Bell alone, something much worse could have happened to her. Yes, what I did was impulsive and maybe even reckless, but I don't regret my actions, and I refuse to feel bad for helping." I pull in a breath and let it out slowly. "I know you don't like me, and I'm okay with that. If you need me to be the villain, there's nothing I can do that will change your opinion of me. But." I lean slightly toward her, and her eyes widen, like she's surprised I'm confronting her. "This isn't really about me. It's about your relationship with your son. I know you love him and he loves you."

Her expression softens slightly, and I continue. "Still, he doesn't deserve to feel bad about taking an opportunity to better his life. He doesn't deserve to feel bad about his decision to move away, even if him moving hurt you." I close my eyes briefly, then lower my voice and look her in the eye. "I know you love him. I understand, because I do too. But you need to see that what you are doing is hurting him."

"I know," she says, and I blink in disbelief. Her acceptance is way too easy. "One day, when you have children of your own, you'll understand just how amazing and difficult it is to watch them grow up and move on with their lives. I love my babies more than anything else in this world. I miss them."

My heart hurts for her, because I can hear pain in her voice. "I'm sorry," I tell her softly.

"No, I am," she replies, looking away briefly. "How I acted toward you yesterday was ridiculous and immature. Tyler is right—I need to grow up before I make my worst nightmare a reality and lose both my kids and my grandbaby." Her face is anguished.

"They love you."

"I haven't made that easy." She sighs, and I take a step toward her.

"Make it easy," I implore her. "Heather needs you now more than ever, especially with everything she's going through. And Tyler needs your support and understanding."

"Heather was right," she says, looking away and pressing her lips together before continuing. "She told me all about you after she and Kennedy visited. She said you were perfect for her brother and that she's never seen him happier." My heart warms at her admission. "I'm sorry, Leah. Truly sorry about yesterday. I hope you can forgive me for the way I acted."

"Already done," I assure her.

She nods; then her expression changes once more, and I hold my breath, not sure what the new look means. "Now. I think we should talk about what happened at the bar." I start to open my mouth to tell her we don't need to, but she cuts me off. "Are you insane?" she asks, sounding just like my mom when she's frustrated with me. "What were you thinking, confronting a drunk man alone?"

I groan, tipping my head back to face the ceiling. "I thought for sure we were past this conversation."

"You put yourself in danger. I understand why you did it, but imagine what would have happened if that man had a knife or a gun."

"You sound just like your son," I tell her, but she doesn't respond to my statement.

She continues talking, like I didn't even speak. "As the future mother of my grandchildren, I expect you to take better care of yourself."

Oh my God, did she just say that?

"You can't go around doing crazy things without thinking about the consequences of your actions, Leah."

"I'll try to do better," I assure her, hoping to end this. As much as I like the fact that she seems to care, I don't want a lecture, especially when I know I'm in for another one from Tyler when he gets back.

"Good. Now. I need to get home and in the kitchen." She starts toward the door. "Thanksgiving dinner isn't going to cook itself, and sadly, Tyler's father is a horrible cook. I can't even trust him to start the water I need to boil the potatoes in."

"Tyler knows how to cook."

"I know." She stops with her hand on the doorknob. "I taught him from an early age how to be self-sufficient. I never wanted him to have to depend on a woman in order to eat. His dad would starve if I weren't around to cook for him. His mom never taught him how to, and I didn't want to make that same mistake with my son."

"You did a good job with him. He's a good man and a really great cook."

"I know." She smiles, looking a little smug, and all I can think is that she and Tyler are seriously a lot alike. "Thank you for talking with me."

"Anytime."

With another nod, she opens the door. "I'll see you and Tyler in a few hours?"

It's a question I can see she was worried to ask. "Yes."

"Good."

She leaves, and I watch her go, then pull in a breath, feeling lighter than I did when I woke up. Tyler might still be mad at me, but at least I know his mom doesn't hate me. I go to the back deck with my cup of coffee and sip on it as I look out at the valley below. When I hear the glass door open, I don't turn to face Tyler, but my body does sag in relief when he fits himself against my back and kisses the top of my head.

"I didn't think you'd be up," he states, sliding his hands around me. "How's your hand feel?"

"It's tight but doesn't hurt too bad, now that I've been using it," I answer, then take a sip of coffee, trying to figure out what to say.

"I'm sorry about last night." He rests the side of his head against mine, and the weight that's been in my stomach all morning dissipates. "I shouldn't have reacted the way I did. I just . . . fuck, the idea of something happening to you makes me feel like I'm coming out of my skin. I don't know what I would've done if he'd touched you. All I could think about last night was what could have happened to you if Bell didn't come tell me what was happening."

"Thankfully, it was okay." I peer over at him.

"Thankfully," he agrees with a sigh. "Just promise me that you won't do anything like that again."

"I hope, really hope, that I'm never in that kind of situation again."

"I notice you didn't promise."

"That's because I won't make a promise I can't keep." I shrug.

He groans, dropping his forehead to my shoulder, and I smile and reach up to pat the back of his head.

"In other news, your mom stopped by while you were gone," I tell him, and his arms tighten while he lifts his head to look at me.

"Please tell me she was nice."

"She came to apologize and to give me a lecture about being crazy and impulsive." I smile at him. "She sounds just like you, or maybe you sound just like her."

"She lectured you?" His brows pull together.

"I believe her exact words were, 'As the future mother of my grand-children, I expect you to take better care of yourself. You can't go around doing crazy things without thinking about the consequences of your actions, Leah.'" I even mimic her tone.

He laughs, and my heart soars at the sound. "Sounds like her," he mutters.

"I like her," I say quietly. "She loves you. I was right—she just misses you and your sister, but she sees that what she's been doing has only pushed the two of you away."

"How long was she here for?"

"Not long. She's kind of direct when she wants to get her point across."

"You're not wrong about that." He kisses the side of my head.

"Are we done fighting?" I ask softly as I set down my mug on the ledge of the deck and turn in his arms.

He frowns down at me. "Pardon?"

"I don't like fighting with you. I didn't like not holding your hand in the truck on the way back to the cabin or going to bed without you last night, and I freaked a little after waking up this morning alone and not finding you in the house."

"We weren't fighting, Leah. Yes, I was pissed, but not at you. I was pissed at the situation and knew I needed time to calm the fuck down and accept that you were okay. When I came up to bed last night after talking to my dad, who heard what happened, you were already asleep. And this morning, you whimpered when you moved your hand, so I knew you were in pain. That's why I got up to go to the store. I wanted you to be able to take something for the pain when you got up."

"I thought you left me."

"What?"

"When I couldn't find you and saw that your truck was gone, I thought you left me."

He frowns. "You thought I just left you here, without us fighting or talking about what happened, without me saying anything at all?" Okay. Now he looks pissed. "Leah, if things ever come to an end between us, baby, you'll know, because before it happens, I'll fight for us, fight for you. I won't just let you walk away, and I hope like fuck that you wouldn't just let me go either. No relationship is ever easy or perfect. We are going to argue, you're gonna piss me off, and I'm gonna return the favor. But at the end of the day, as long as neither of us gives up fighting, we will make it work."

"You're really good at relationship stuff."

"As you pointed out, I've had some practice," he jokes, and my nose scrunches up at the reminder. He leans in, kissing the tip of it while chuckling. His smile leaves, and he takes my face between his hands. "I've learned over time what I want, what I don't want, and exactly the kind of woman I'm looking for. I know each man you dated before me taught you those same things."

"You're right," I agree while leaning closer to him. "I'm sorry I made you worried last night, and I know what I did was stupid. I just had to."

His fingers skim along my jaw. "What you did just confirmed why I'd be stupid not to want to spend the rest of my life with you."

Did he just say that? What?

"You care about people, even people you don't know. You want everyone around you to be happy, and you have a way of making that happen for them. You see the good in the world when most people are so jaded they'd complain about rain that's coming in two days when it's sunny outside." I melt deeper into him as my heart starts to pound in a strange tempo and my eyes start to water. "I love that you're optimistic and impulsive. I love that you love me enough that you were willing to ignore your own worries about coming to meet my family and do it anyway, because you knew I wanted you here with me. I love the look on your face when I get home, and the way you are with your niece and nephews. I love how you treated Heather like you'd known her for ages, and the look on your face every time Kennedy laughed."

His voice gentles as tears fall and start running down my cheeks. "Really, I just love you."

I can't respond by telling him all the reasons I love him, because a sob rips from my chest, cutting off anything I might say. I close my arms around him as he tightens his grip around me, and I rest the side of my head against his chest. When one of his hands slides my T-shirt up and his warm hand meets nothing but skin, he curses, and I freeze.

"Fuck, baby, it's cold out, and you've got nothing on." He pulls back, and I watch through watery eyes as he looks down at my bare feet. "Not even shoes."

I let out a squeak as he lifts me suddenly off the ground to hold me tightly against him. "I'm not cold," I reply. He grunts something under his breath I can't make out as he carries me inside through the sliding glass door.

Once we reach the couch, he pulls the throw off the back of it and shakes it out before wrapping it around me and then tucking it under my legs. "It's not even fifty degrees out," he informs me. He goes back outside and returns with my mug. He dumps the probably cold coffee in the sink, then pours me a fresh cup and stirs in milk and sugar. "Drink this. You need to warm up," he orders, handing me the mug, and I wrap my hands around it, sighing as it warms up my fingers.

He goes to the temperature-control panel on the wall and taps the up arrow before going to the fireplace and flipping the switch next to it. What looks like a real fire roars to life in an instant as the electric fireplace comes on. When he comes back to the couch, he lifts my legs before he sits, then settles my feet on his lap and captures them with his hands. "Your feet are freezing."

I shiver and my toes curl. I take a sip of hot coffee to distract myself from the fact that I do feel cold now. Actually, I'm freezing. After I swallow, I shake my head. "I honestly didn't feel cold before."

"You were distracted. Now that you're not, your body is registering that you were outside in nothing but a T-shirt without even shoes on your feet," he states, rubbing my feet. "We should take a shower."

Him naked in the shower with me? I'm totally okay with that idea.

"I think that would be good," I say a little breathlessly.

Reading the look I give him, he shakes his head and gets up. After he lifts me into his arms, he looks down at me. "I guess if a shower is the only way to warm you up, I can endure it."

"Thanks," I say before I nip the edge of his jaw. When he groans, I smile, then do a happy dance in my head as he takes me to the shower to warm me up in the best way possible.

"I'm so tired." I cover my mouth with my hand as I yawn.

"Almost there." Tyler laughs as he smiles down at me and helps me up the few steps of my front porch to my front door.

We left Tennessee later today than we planned to. After Thanksgiving dinner—which was spent with Tyler's family and a few of their close friends—we spent the rest of our time in Tennessee with his mom and dad. His mom did a one-eighty toward me after our talk, and I loved getting to know her and his dad. Really, I enjoyed watching Tyler with them, since he has the same close relationship with them that I have with my own parents.

I found out that his dad is funny and a tad bit sarcastic, and his mom is doting and forever waiting on the men in her life. Not that she seemed to mind. She actually seemed to enjoy taking care of them. Our plan to leave early Sunday morning was waylaid when Tyler's grandmother, who'd heard about me from his mom, flew in from Florida on Saturday evening and insisted on having lunch with us before we left on Sunday. We didn't leave Tennessee until almost four. Now it's almost eleven at night, and I'm ready to fall on my face.

"How are you not tired?" I ask Tyler as he uses his key to open the door. "I didn't even drive, and I'm exhausted."

"You bought me a huge coffee at the gas station to keep me awake and my bladder full," he reminds me.

"Oh . . . right," I reply, and he grins. As soon as the door's open, I stumble in and go directly to the coat closet. I open it before I start to slip off my coat. "Tomorrow when I get off work, I'll go pick up Bruce and Mouse and bring them home."

"What the fuck?" Tyler barks, and I turn to look at him over my shoulder. When I see the horrified look on his face, I follow his gaze across the room.

That's when I see the red writing on the wall, spelling out the word *WHORE* in big, bold lettering. I pull my eyes off the word and glance around my house, seeing the place is completely trashed. How did I not see that when I came in? The cushions on my couch are slashed, with white fuzz poking out of the fabric. My flat-screen TV is lying facedown on the ground; the back is bent inward and looks like it's been stomped on. Broken glass, pictures from the walls, and dirt from my potted plants lie scattered across the wood floors and around the room.

"What happened?" I whisper in shock and disbelief, my mind trying to play catch-up as I take everything in.

"Come on." Tyler grabs my hand. He pulls me out of the living room and through the front door behind him, and then he picks me up and carries me down the steps when I start to stumble.

"Who did that?" I ask as he carries me across the grass toward his house.

"I don't know." He sets me on my feet to unlock his door. When he lets us inside his house and flips on the light, I expect to see his place in the same state as mine, but it isn't. It's clean and just the way he left it a few days ago. "Sit, baby," he orders, forcing me to sit on the couch. "I'm going to go back over to your place to call the cops."

"What? No!" I practically scream as I stand up and latch on to his arm. "What if someone's still in there? Please," I beg. "Don't leave me. Just call the cops from here."

He studies me for a moment before he nods and wraps his arms around me. He pulls out his phone, and I listen to him dial 911, then tell the person on the phone that my house was broken into. He gives my address, along with his. I hear them tell him that it will be about five minutes before officers show up and that we should wait where we are while they do a walk-through of the house. Then, once it's clear, they'll come over and get us.

When Tyler hangs up, I let go of the hold I have on him and take a seat on the couch. I think out loud as I lean forward, resting my elbows on my knees and my face in my hands. "Who would do that? Who would break into my house and write something like that on the wall?"

I don't get it. I don't have enemies or an ex who's crazy enough to do something like that. Heck, until that guy at the bar a few nights ago, I'd never even been in a fight in my life.

"It's probably just some punk kids fucking around and being stupid." Tyler sits down next to me. He rubs my back and attempts to comfort me. "Maybe they saw you haven't been home for a few days and—"

I cut him off as I turn my head to look at him. "They wrote *whore* on my wall and slashed my couch. You haven't been home for a few days, either, and they didn't break in here and destroy your place. I mean, if they'd just trashed my house and stole stuff, I might agree with you about the stupid-kid theory." I give a short jerk of my head. "But that word on my wall makes it seem personal, like they have something against me. My TV is worth a few hundred dollars at a pawn shop, and they didn't take it—they broke it."

"Do you have an idea of who might have done something like that?" he asks gently.

"No," I deny with another jerky shake of my head. "I don't know anyone who has anything against me." I rest my face in my hands once more and try to think of someone I've pissed off, but no one comes to mind.

About ten minutes later, there's a knock on Tyler's door. Two police officers are standing outside when he answers, and they come inside and ask me a few questions before they escort Tyler and me over to my house.

As we walk through each room, I see that nothing of importance is missing, but everything is in ruins. The little jewelry I own is still in the unopened box on my dresser, but my bedding is in tatters, along with my mattress. Every piece of clothing I own is strewed across the room, pulled from hangers and out of drawers. In my bathroom, drawers are pulled out of their slots, the contents dumped on the floor, and the shower curtain is ripped, hanging by just a few hooks. The kitchen is in the same shape. Dishes are broken, layering the floor, and food from the fridge has been thrown around the room.

When Tyler pulls me into his chest and whispers softly in my ear, I realize I'm crying.

"We're going to put up tape and pull prints tomorrow morning," I hear one of the officers say. "Hopefully, whoever did this didn't wear gloves and left something behind."

"Yeah, hopefully," Tyler rumbles, holding my head firmly against his chest as he sifts his fingers through my hair.

"Is she good to stay with you?"

"She's good," he agrees before he lifts me into his arms.

He talks with the officers some more, but I don't register anything they're saying. My mind is overwhelmed with everything that's happened and the state of my house. I feel numb, like I'm in an insane dream I can't wake up from. It isn't until Tyler lays me in his bed and wraps himself around me that I start to come back to myself.

My chest aches. "Why? Why would someone do something like that?"

"I don't know, baby," he answers, holding me tightly while resting his lips on the back of my head. I shiver in his hold as fear creeps down my spine. "You're safe, Leah. Nothing and no one will ever touch you."

I want to believe him, but part of me knows he might be wrong.

Suggestion 15

BE THANKFUL

LEAH

"Did they tell you what time they'd be over to lift prints?" my mom asks, handing me a cup of coffee before taking a seat next to me on Tyler's couch.

"Thanks." I take a sip before I answer. "No, just that they'd call when they got here so I could let them in."

"I told you that you needed to get an alarm system put in," my dad says, sounding pissed, and I look to where he's standing near the door with his arms crossed over his chest. He's been an angry papa bear since he got here, mad that I waited until this morning to call and tell them about the break-in, since I didn't want them worrying all night. My dad was not happy and insisted on coming right over, even though I explained to him that I wasn't allowed into my house until the cops told me it was okay. My mom was just as upset about it and came with him.

"Gary," Mom sighs, and Dad cuts his eyes to her.

"A girl living on her own needs an alarm system or a dog. You don't have either. Instead, you have a fucking cat that can't even be seen most of the time," Dad grumbles.

Mom defends me, glaring at my dad. "Mouse is with Mom, and Tyler and Leah weren't even here. I doubt this would've happened if they were, because Bruce would've been around. Just thank God she's okay. You can complain later."

"I'm not complaining. I'm pointing out that if she had an alarm system, it would've been armed while she was gone, and the cops would've been notified when someone broke in. This could have been avoided." He shakes his head, then glares at me. "I'm calling and having a system installed today."

"Dad." I sigh in frustration.

"And I'm telling them to put one in here, too, since you're staying here."

"This is Tyler's house, not Leah's," Mom snaps at him. "You can't just order Tyler to put in a security system because you deem it so."

"I was going to put one in anyway," Tyler states, coming out of the bedroom where he went to get changed for work. "Gary's right. Leah is here with me, and I need a system. So does she." He looks at my dad. "I hate that I gotta leave right now, but I'd appreciate if you made the call to have the system installed today. Let them know I'll pay extra if they need me to. I just want it done by this evening."

"I'll get it done," Dad assures him, looking relieved.

Tyler lifts his chin, then looks at me. "Are you going to be okay? I don't want to go, but I need to check on the job. I won't be gone long—maybe two hours."

"I'll be fine." I feel guilty that he's worried about me when he needs to be thinking about work. "Mom and Dad are here, and after I hear from the cops, I might go to the shop. I need to call the clients I was supposed to see today and reschedule appointments."

"All right, baby." He comes closer, dropping a kiss on my lips. "Let me know what the cops say, and don't forget to call your insurance company. They need to know what happened so you can file a claim with them."

"I'll make sure she calls them," Mom says, giving my hand a squeeze.

Tyler glances at her and nods before looking at me once more. "Love you."

"Love you too." I close my eyes as his lips touch my forehead, and then I watch him leave after saying goodbye to my parents.

"I need caffeine," Dad states as he goes to the kitchen to get a cup of coffee. While he's in there, I hear him on the phone, scheduling an appointment to have security systems put in at Tyler's place and mine.

"You okay, honey?" Mom asks softly, and I look over at her. I'm not okay, but I can't think about that right now. I need to deal with the cops and then start cleaning up my house after they do what they need to do. "I should have come over to check on things while you were gone."

"I'm glad you didn't," I tell her. "It's bad enough what they did to my house. I don't want to think about anyone I care about walking in on them and what could have happened then. I just hope the cops find something and are able to catch the person who did it." I lean my head back against the couch.

"I hope so too," she agrees, then lets out a sigh when her cell phone dings. She quickly picks it up and starts typing.

"Is everything okay?"

"Just a client. She's upset that I canceled her appointment."

"I'm sorry you're missing work."

"I'm not." She drops her phone to the coffee table and looks at me. "You're my baby. There is nowhere else I need to be right now. My clients will either understand or they can find a different stylist."

"Like that's going to happen." I roll my eyes at her. People wait months to get an appointment with my mom. No way will they move on to someone else just because of a delay.

"All right, installers will be here in a few hours to put in the security system here, and as soon as the cops say you're allowed to go back into your house, they'll put in a system there as well."

"How much is this going to cost me?" I ask him. I have some money saved, but I've been working hard to pay off the student loan I still have from nursing school.

"Nothing." Dad takes a seat in the chair next to the fireplace. "Consider it a Christmas gift."

"Oh my, it's just what I wanted," I reply sarcastically, and he and Mom laugh. "Let me guess—you're getting Mom a vacuum for Christmas."

"If your dad buys me a vacuum for Christmas, he's moving in with you," Mom says, and I grin at her.

"I thought you wanted that Roomba thing," Dad mutters, looking a little worried.

Oh no. He really did buy her a vacuum for Christmas. I was just joking.

"I do want one, but not as a Christmas gift." She narrows her eyes on him. "Did you buy me that for Christmas?"

"Of course not."

"Yeah, Mom. Of course not." I start to laugh, and Dad grumbles under his breath. My cell phone on the table rings, and I pick it up. When I see a local number, I answer, then sigh in relief and look at my dad. "The cops are next door. Can you take them my key so they can go in?"

"Of course, honey," he says, and I tell the person on the phone that someone will be right over, then hang up. My dad grabs my key off the counter and leaves, returning just a few minutes later. "They said it won't take long, and they'll come over to get you when they're finished to take you over."

"I should call my insurance company. I need to find out exactly what they're going to need from me in order for me to file a claim."

"Do that now. Hopefully, by the time you're done, they'll be finished up next door," Mom says.

"Right." I get up and take my cell phone with me to the kitchen. I grab a piece of paper and a pen and then lean against the counter to make the call. I explain to the agent on the phone what happened, then write down exactly what I need to do. As I'm getting off the phone, there's a knock on the door, and my mom goes to answer it. I expect to see the cops, so I'm surprised when I see Chrissie.

"Oh my God, are you okay?" she asks when she spots me in the kitchen. "I just got your message and came right over. I can't believe this."

"I'm fine." I wrap my arms around her. "Who's working at the shop?" I ask when she lets me go. Most of her employees are high school students, and school is not out for the day.

"I have this fancy little *Closed* sign and used it."

I groan, feeling guilty. I hate that everyone is missing work because of this. "You didn't have to do that."

"Yeah, I did." She rests her hands on her hips. "I wanted to see for myself that you were okay and to help clean up."

"Thanks." I give in because I know, just like my mom and dad, that she won't be swayed. And the truth is I need all the help I can get. My house is trashed. It's going to take a few days to get all the garbage out and a couple more to get everything cleaned up and organized again.

"Wow, that was easy. Are you feeling okay?"

"Shut up." I roll my eyes and head for the couch. "We have to wait for the officers to come get us before we can go to my place. Hopefully, it won't be much longer."

"Well, while we wait, I want to hear all about your trip. How did it go?"

"Ooh, I want to know too," Mom inserts, looking excited.

Dad stands up and comes over to me and kisses the top of my head. "I'm going to go outside and wait on the porch."

"You don't want to hear about my trip?"

"No," he states firmly, and I laugh as he leans over to kiss my mom before heading outside.

"All right, your dad's gone. Tell us everything."

I look between my mom and my best friend, then tell them everything. About meeting Tyler's mom for the first time and how horribly that went. About going to the bar and getting in a fight. About thinking Tyler had left me. About the talk with his mom and her acceptance of me. Then about lunch with his grandma. When I'm done, both Chrissie's and Mom's mouths are hanging open.

"How long were you there for?" Chrissie asks, and I smile at her.

"Just the long weekend."

"You were busy," she mumbles.

"You're not wrong," I mumble back, and she laughs.

Mom reaches over, resting her hand on my knee and gaining my attention. "You and Tyler's mom are okay now, right?"

"We're okay now," I assure her, and then I look at the door when it opens.

"Ready to go?" Dad asks as he pokes his head inside.

"Yep."

When we all get outside, two officers lead us over to my house. They explain what they did and how long it will take for them to get the prints into the system. They seem hopeful about their findings, which makes me feel a little better. After they leave, I do a walk-through of the house with Chrissie and my parents, and they're all visibly upset but glad I wasn't here.

After I assure them I'm okay, we go to the kitchen and start to clean the food off the walls and floor before it starts to stink or mold. When Tyler shows up, he tells me that some of his guys are coming with their trucks to help him get rid of furniture and stuff that's no longer usable. My mom, Chrissie, and I fill bags in my kitchen, and my dad and Tyler drag my couch and mattress outside so it will be easier to remove them later.

While we're cleaning, the security system installers show up, and they work quickly to put in the systems at Tyler's house and mine. They run through how to use them and what will happen if the alarm is triggered. I'm a little overwhelmed by the complicated system, but I don't admit it, because they make it seem like a child could figure it out. Once they leave, I attempt to scrub the word *whore* off the wall. Since they used ketchup to write the word, it's left a stain that will have to be painted over.

Five hours later, tired, sweaty, and hungry, I look around my living room at my best friend, my parents, and my brothers—who came over when they got off work—and watch them haul the last of the garbage outside. I glance across to Tyler, his guys Jake and Mike, and Scott, who are in the process of seeing if the TV might still work, and let out a deep breath. Because of all of them helping clean and haul garbage to the local dump, my house is just about back to normal. I still need to wash my clothes and put them away and then get a couch and a new mattress, but for the most part, things look like they did before I left. I thought it would take me days to clean everything up, but with everyone's help, it's just about done.

"If I had millions of dollars, I'd buy you each a car or a house or whatever you wanted," I say, and everyone turns to look at me. "Thank you." I wave a hand around the room. "I don't even know how to tell you how grateful I am for all your help."

"Think you just did, sweetheart," Scott says, smiling. "Though if you were a millionaire, I'd ask for Jet Skis."

"I'll remember that if I ever win the lotto," I reply, and he grins at me before turning back to the TV just as it suddenly comes to life.

"It still works." I grab the remote off the side table resting against the wall and flip through the channels. "I can't believe it's working."

"If I were you, I'd still put it in my claim with the insurance company," Jake says, looking from the TV to me. "I know it works now, but it could stop working in a day or a week, and you don't want to have to pay out of pocket if you don't need to."

"You're probably right," I agree as Tyler walks across the room toward me. Once he's close, he wraps his arm around my shoulders and kisses the side of my head. I tip my head back to look up at him and whisper, "Thank you."

"You know you don't have to thank me," he whispers back; then he leans down, touching his mouth to mine. The front door opens, and I turn to see who's coming in. I grin from ear to ear when Bruce bounces into the room, heading right for Tyler and me with his tail going a hundred miles a minute.

"You're home!" I wrap my arms around his furry neck and laugh as he licks my face. "I missed you too," I tell him while standing to greet Angie as she comes inside with my brother.

"I thought about keeping him, but you know where I live, so I didn't think it would work," she informs me, and I laugh as she gives me a hug. "I'm so sorry about what happened."

"Me too," I say as she lets me go to accept a hug from Tyler. "Where are the boys?"

"With Beth. I didn't want them to get freaked. Noah told me that things were pretty bad." She glances around. "I guess you guys got everything cleaned up."

"We did, but I still wouldn't know how to explain to them about my missing couch, so it's probably good they aren't here."

"True," she responds, then looks between Tyler and me. "Do they know who could have done this?"

"Not yet. They said it will take a few days before they're even able to get the prints into the system to do a search. Hopefully, we'll know something soon," I tell her as Tyler's cell phone rings. I watch him walk off with his phone to his ear, and then I turn to ask if anyone wants pizza. I stop when Tyler comes back, looking furious.

"What happened?" Scott asks.

"That was Detective Miller. He said that when he got to the office today, he heard my name mentioned along with the break-in here. When the officers who took the prints got back to the station, he asked them if he could have a look at them, and on a whim he compared the partial he collected during the arson investigation to the prints they pulled today."

"They got a match?" my dad guesses, and I look at him, then back to Tyler.

No way.

"They got a match," Tyler agrees.

"But . . . but that doesn't make any sense. Why would someone set a fire at your storage unit and then weeks later trash my house?"

"I don't know, baby," he says, running his fingers through his hair. "Detective Miller wants me to take you down to the station to ask you some questions."

My chest gets tight, and nausea turns my empty stomach. "Why? Does he think I had something to do with what happened?"

Tyler's expression softens, and he comes closer to me, wrapping a hand around the back of my neck. "No, he just wants to see if there's anyone you might suspect, anyone you've made mad or fought with recently."

"There is no one."

"Talking with him might lead him somewhere, might give him a clue."

"But they have a full print. Can't they just put that in the system and see if it matches someone?"

"No, unfortunately, just because they have a match doesn't mean they're going to be able to rush the process. And in the meantime, Detective Miller doesn't want something to happen again."

"You need to go talk with him," Dad inserts, and I pull in a shaky breath.

I know he's right, that they are right. I need to go talk to him. I just don't want to. I now feel like I'm somehow the cause of all this, but I don't understand how that could be possible. I don't have any enemies that I know of. I've never even cut someone in line or sneezed without covering my mouth. I get along with everyone I meet. It just doesn't make any sense. "Okay, I'll go talk to him. I just need to shower and change first."

"I'll walk you over to my place so you can do that; then we'll go," Tyler says.

I nod at him and look around the room. "Thank you all again," I say, then listen to their sweet replies. I hug my parents, Chrissie, Angie, and my brothers. Tyler walks me to his house, with Bruce coming with us, and I take a shower and get dressed while he talks to his parents and fills them in on what's going on. He's standing in the bathroom, watching my every move with worry-filled eyes. By the time I'm done getting ready, my earlier hunger is nowhere in sight, and my nerves are a mess.

"It's going to be okay," Tyler says as he opens the door and helps me into his truck. "You're not in trouble. You're just answering a few questions."

"I know, but now I feel like this is all my fault."

"It's not. Whoever's doing this is obviously sick and in need of help. That's not on you."

"I just keep trying to think of someone, anyone, I've upset, but no one's coming to mind," I tell him, letting out a frustrated hiss when I can't seem to get the seat belt to work.

He takes the buckle from me, then slides it around my waist and latches it in place. "Breathe for me and relax, baby. It's going to be okay." He kisses my forehead, then steps back and slams the door. As he comes around the driver's side, I take a few deep breaths to relax. It works, and I settle back against my seat. When he gets behind the wheel, he grabs my hand, placing it against his thigh before turning on his truck and backing out of his driveway. "Have you had anything more than coffee today?" he asks me, and I turn to look at him before I answer.

"No, there wasn't time, not with my parents showing up and everything else that happened."

"We'll stop on the way and grab you a sandwich," he says as he rests his hand over mine.

"I don't think I can eat right now." Even the thought of food makes my stomach turn.

"You're gonna eat something, even if I have to force-feed you," he informs me, turning to look at me when he stops at a red light.

When I see the determined look in his eyes, I grumble, "Fine."

"Also, Mom and Dad are worried. They're driving up the day after tomorrow to spend a few days with us."

"What?" I cry. "I don't want them here, not if someone's really trying to hurt me."

He ignores me and continues. "I placed an order for a mattress for your bed this afternoon. It should be delivered by tomorrow evening. We'll stay at your place and let my parents have mine while they're in town."

"I don't like that, Tyler. If someone's trying to hurt me, your family could end up caught up in things. That's not okay with me."

"Would you have any luck convincing your parents or brothers to stay away?" he asks. No, I wouldn't; even if I told them not to come around until the person who broke into my house was caught, they would ignore me. "You don't even have to answer that question. I know the answer. They want to make sure we're okay, that *you* are okay."

"I still don't like it."

"Sorry, baby. It's not something you need to like, just something you're going to have to deal with. Besides, this will give our families a chance to meet."

"Great," I sigh. "I'm so happy about the idea of everyone coming together since some lunatic has something against me. I mean, could there ever be a better time for our families to get together? I think not," I say sarcastically while shaking my head.

"Everyone will be coming together because they care about you and want to see that you're okay."

"You can keep saying that, but it doesn't change the fact that I might be putting the people I love and care about in danger. I mean, heck, someone lit your storage space on fire, then broke into my house, trashed the place, and wrote *whore* on the wall. I don't even want to think about what they might do next."

"I will not let anything fucking happen to you."

"You might not have a say. You can't be with me twenty-four hours a day, seven days a week. You have to work, and so do I. I don't know who's targeting me or why."

"Stop!" he roars, and I clamp my mouth shut, feeling like an idiot. I know he's worried, and me acting crazy isn't going to help that. "No one is going to fucking hurt you. No one is going to get near you, and I don't give a fuck if I have to stand guard over you for the next . . ." He jerks his fingers through his hair. "For the next however long it takes for the cops to find who did this shit."

"Okay," I whisper when I see his chest rising and falling quickly. "You're right. I'm just freaked. No one's going to do anything to me." I rub his thigh, hoping to calm him down. "I'm sorry. I just . . . I'm just overthinking things and being stupid."

"You're not stupid." He pulls in to park in front of one of the local sandwich shops. "It's not stupid that you're worried. You have a reason to be worried, but I need you to believe I will never let anything harm you."

"I believe you," I state, looking into his eyes when he turns his head toward me. I do believe him. I know he would step in front of a bullet to protect me. That he would risk his own life to save mine. I just hope that never ever happens.

"Good." His fingers give mine a gentle squeeze. "Now let's get you something to eat, get the shit with Miller over with, and then get home, where I can fuck away all thoughts about everything that's happened."

I really like that idea. I don't say that; instead, I lean toward him and kiss his jaw. "I love you," I tell him before I move back, unhook my belt, and get out of his truck.

After we eat, he takes me to the police station, where I meet with Detective Miller. Calvin Miller, to be precise. A man who also happens to be tall, fit, and seriously hot, with dark-brown hair and stunning blue eyes. I feel comfortable with him immediately. He never makes me feel like I'm being interrogated. He doesn't ask me question after question; he just talks to me about my life and the people in it while he writes in his notebook.

When we're done, he tells me that he will do everything within his power to put the person or persons behind bars, and for some reason, having him on the case makes me feel better.

When Tyler takes me home to his place, he wastes no time in making me forget about everything but the two of us. And when I fall asleep against his chest, listening to the sound of his heart, I'm no longer worried, because I know the guy with his arms wrapped around me will protect me.

Suggestion 16

JUST SAY YES

LEAH

I lean forward and adjust the temperature, then the air vents. I sit back and then forward again to change the station on the radio. Once I find something worth listening to, I pick up my purse and dig through it.

"Relax." Tyler chuckles, and I turn my head to glare at him.

"Don't tell me to relax when I'm about to sit through a fancy dinner with your family and mine," I huff, flipping down the visor and swiping on lip gloss.

The night before last, his parents arrived close to midnight. They were exhausted from the drive, so we helped them get settled at his house and told them we'd see them in the morning, but only for a bit. Both Tyler and I still had to work. We had breakfast with them on Thursday morning, and while we were eating, Tyler suggested that our families get together Friday. Then he proceeded to call my mom to ask her to make reservations for all of us. Of course my mom was happy to set things up; I just wasn't as happy as she was. I wanted the first meeting of our parents to be much more casual and personal. Lord only knows what my grams might say or even what one of my brothers might do.

"It's just dinner, baby." He shrugs, and I narrow my eyes on his profile.

"I know, but I . . . I just wanted our parents to meet alone. We could've had my parents over, or—"

He cuts me off. "You still don't have a couch. And I don't have a dining room table. I figured dinner out would be the easiest for everyone."

"You need to buy a dining room table," I say with a sigh while adjusting the top of my dress. A little black dress I bought to wear to dinner with him. I just never expected our parents, my siblings, their spouses, and my niece and nephews to be with us when we went out to said dinner.

"I'll get right on that after I finish paying off our new alarm systems and the fence they're currently putting in my backyard."

Wait . . . what?

"My dad said he was going to pay for my alarm system," I say quietly.

"Yeah, and then I told him he wouldn't be."

"I have some money. Just let me—"

"No." He shakes his head in denial, the fricking stubborn caveman.

"Tyler," I hiss.

"No, Leah, I'm good, and if you think I need a table in my dining room that we never fucking use, then we'll go out and buy one tomorrow when I get off work. But." He glances over at me. "Before that happens, I think we need to figure out which of our houses we're keeping. Mine is more updated, but you've got an unfinished basement that would add to the square footage if I finished it out and added a bathroom down there."

"What?" I breathe, my mind trying to play catch-up with the weight of our conversation. "Are you saying we should move in together?"

"Baby, we basically live together now. It makes no sense for us to be paying two mortgages each month. We could be saving that money."

"Holy cow."

I feel him look at me. "Did you really expect us to be neighbors for the rest of our lives and not move in together one day?" He laughs.

Did I? I'm not sure. I've been living in the moment with him and taking each day as it comes. I know I love him and that he loves me, but until right now, I've never considered what our future might look like. He wants us to live together, and that means eventually we might get married and have babies. I know he said that to his mom, but I didn't really think much about it at the time, because it seemed like something that wouldn't be happening for years to come. Apparently that's not the case.

"Holy cow," I repeat, and he laughs even louder as he pulls into the parking lot for the restaurant and parks his truck in an empty spot.

When he shuts down the engine, he turns to face me, then reaches over, picks up my hand, and pulls me closer. "I think we should move into your place since you have more square footage, and with a little work, it would be worth more money in the long run." His eyes search mine. "I'll fix up the kitchen, remodel the master bathroom, and finish off the basement. When we have a baby, you have a room down the hall that we can turn into a nursery."

A baby. Oh my God. I think I might start hyperventilating.

"We don't have to sell my house right away," he says, searching my eyes. "We can rent it out until you're ready for us to let it go."

"I'm ready." I close my eyes and drop my forehead to his chin. "I . . . I want to live with you. I want to start a life with you. I don't care where we live. I don't even care if you want to move back to Tennessee. I'll follow you wherever you go."

"Baby."

"My home is you. Wherever you are is where I belong, the only place I belong."

"Fuck . . . I wasn't . . . shit, I wasn't going to do this now. I was going to wait until we had our families around to do it, but fuck it."

Having no idea what he's talking about, I pull my head back in confusion to look at him. Then I watch him dig into the pocket of his slacks. His eyes fill with relief when he finds whatever he's looking for. When he grabs my left hand and holds it between us, I drop my eyes forward and watch his fingers as they run over mine.

"Tyler," I whisper as confused excitement fills my stomach.

"I love you, Leah." My eyes fly up, and I look into his. "I love you more than anything in this world. I can't imagine waking up without you by my side every day, and I fucking hope I'll never have to." My heart pounds when I notice the shimmer of something glittering between his fingers, and then my world seems to come to a stop when I recognize it's a ring—a beautiful ring with a thick gold band and an oval-shaped diamond. "Marry me, baby. Marry me and make me the happiest man in the world."

"Yes," I whisper, and he slides the breathtaking ring onto my finger. "Oh my God, yes." I laugh, wrapping my arms around him and holding on tight.

"Thank God."

I laugh harder. "Did you really think there was any chance I would say no?"

"I wasn't sure. You seemed pretty shocked about the idea of us living together, when we've been doing that for a while," he says, pulling back to look at me.

"It takes me a while to catch up." I grin.

"I see that." He grins back before his eyes drop to my hand.

When his thumb touches the edge of the diamond, tears fill my eyes. "I can't believe this is real, that you're real," I breathe, and he looks up at the same time I do. "I never thought I would be this happy or this excited about the future. I can't wait to spend the rest of my life with you." I lean forward and press my mouth against his. "Thank you," I tell him, then jump when someone pounds on the window behind Tyler, startling me.

I peek around his shoulder and smile at his mom, whose face is pressed to the glass. "Are you two coming in or staying out here?" she asks when Tyler rolls down the window.

"We're coming. Just give us a minute."

"I've given you ten minutes," she informs him, and then she looks at me. "Remember, we followed you here."

"Ma, I need a couple more minutes with my fiancée," he says, and I see the moment his statement registers. Her eyes widen, and I lift my hand toward her, watching tears fill her eyes.

"Oh my God, I'm going to cry." She covers her mouth while holding my hand. "I'm so happy for you two."

"What's the holdup?" Tyler's dad asks, and then his eyes drop to my hand, which his wife is still holding, and he grins. "Congrats, you two."

"Thank you." I smile at both of them.

"We'll give you a few more minutes." His mom wipes at her cheeks as his dad shakes his head and wraps his arms around her.

"Thanks, Mom," Tyler murmurs, watching them walk off before he rolls the window back up. "We should head inside. Your mom and dad knew I planned on asking you to marry me tonight. Your mom will want to see the ring; she never got a chance to before."

"My parents knew?"

"I'm southern, baby. I couldn't ask you without asking your dad for permission."

"Right."

"And it's the twenty-first century, so I had to ask your mom as well."

"I'm sure she loved that."

"I know your family means everything to you. I wanted to make sure they were okay with the idea."

"Were they?" I question. I know he and I haven't been together long. I'm not sure if my parents care, but they might think it's too soon.

"You'll have to show them the ring and find out." He leans forward, brushing his lips over mine, before asking, "Ready?"

"Definitely." I get out of the truck, and his parents come over. I give both of them a hug as they offer congratulations; then we all walk through the parking lot and into the restaurant together.

As soon as we get inside, the hostess leads us to a table, where my family is already seated. When my parents spot us, they both stand, and I smile at them, then lift my left hand facing out and wiggle my ring finger. My mom screams at the top of her lungs and rushes through the quiet restaurant toward us, and my dad shakes his head while smiling proudly. I laugh, holding on to Tyler's hand tightly, as everyone gets up to hug us and make introductions.

When we all settle into our seats, I feel Tyler's fingers tighten almost painfully around mine. I look at him, then follow his gaze to where Charles is seated a couple of tables away with a beautiful blonde. As his eyes meet mine, he smiles tightly at me, then looks at Tyler and gives him a hate-filled look.

"Just ignore him," I tell Tyler, and he looks down at me. "I haven't even heard from him or seen him since that day at the salon. He doesn't exist."

His jaw clenches, and then he mutters, "You're right," before kissing me gently.

When he leans away, I glance at Charles's table, and a feeling of unease slides down my spine when I see his eyes on me. I look away and then avoid looking at his table as dinner progresses.

"Who is that guy?" Tyler's mom asks, leaning toward me.

"Pardon?"

"That guy at that other table." She nods in the direction of Charles and his date. "He hasn't stopped looking over here."

"I went to dinner with him once." I let out a sigh.

"Just once?" She looks confused. "You'd think you were supposed to marry him by the way he's looking over here. Even his date is annoyed," she says, and I look at Tyler when he starts to shove back from the table.

"Where are you going?" I ask, grabbing on to his arm.

"I'm going to convince him that he needs to keep his eyes off you," he growls.

"Stop," I beg, and he studies me for a moment before he pulls in one breath and then another. I know he's attempting to get himself under control. "Please just ignore him."

"Baby." His jaw clenches.

"I think he's coming over here," his mom whispers, and my head flies up. When I see that Charles is, in fact, coming toward us, my stomach starts to sink.

"What the fuck?" Tyler rumbles, and I hold on to his arm even tighter, thinking he's going to get up and kick Charles's ass. But then I notice he's looking toward the entrance of the restaurant, at Detective Miller and two uniformed officers coming our way.

"What's going on?" I ask as the cops split up at our table, walk around it, and close in on Charles.

"Leah, Tyler." Detective Miller stops behind us, resting his hands on his hips as he watches the cops put cuffs on Charles. "I planned on calling you this evening to let you know I was able to track down the person we think is responsible for the fire and the break-in," he says.

I look over at Charles in disbelief. Him. He's the one. I shake my head as the officers start to lead him away.

"Get your fucking hands off me. I want a fucking lawyer!" he shouts.

"Are you saying Charles set the fire and trashed my house?" I can't believe this. It doesn't even make sense. We dated years ago and had only one recent date. I scrub my hands down my face as my family gets closer.

"Can we step outside? I'd like to explain what's happened," Miller says, and Tyler helps me up, then tells everyone we'll be back. When we get outside, we walk away from where anyone might hear us talk. Tyler settles me against his side with his arm around my shoulders, and Miller stands in front of us with his hands tucked into his jeans.

"Charles didn't personally set the fire or trash your house. He had the grandson of a client of his do it. He told the kid that he would throw his grandmother's case if he didn't do what he asked. His grandmother needs around-the-clock care that, without the money from winning that claim, they would never be able to afford. The kid didn't know any better, thought he didn't have a choice, so he agreed. At first the kid didn't think things would be bad, but when he asked him to get rid of your dog, he freaked. He told me he couldn't do it, that the dog was cool, so he just took off his collar and then called the ASPCA to pick him up."

"Oh my God," I whisper, and Tyler's arm tightens.

"When Charles asked him to set the fire, he did it, but he didn't think the place would burn like it did."

"And then he had him trash Leah's house. What the fuck was the point of all this?" Tyler barks.

"He never told him what his issue was with Leah. He just told him what he wanted done." Miller looks at me. "What was your relationship with him? I know you mentioned him when we spoke."

"We dated when we were much younger," I say. "It didn't work out, but like I said, we were young. We went on one date a while back, but I didn't go out with him again after that." I'm having a hard time wrapping my head around the fact that Charles is the one behind the fire and the break-in at my place.

"He was pissed," Tyler snarls, then pulls in a breath. "Leah and I got together not long after they had their date. She didn't tell him that she wasn't interested, but she never called him or messaged him after either. His ego couldn't handle the idea of her not wanting him, and he obviously lost his fucking mind. Please tell me he's going to jail."

"Knowing how much money he has and who his dad is, I'm going to be honest. He will probably be out in a couple hours without any real charges against him. What I have on him is not much, and it's his word against a kid who's been in jail before for robbery and theft. I know he did it, you know he did it, and tonight, everyone in the restaurant saw him get arrested. Those people are all going to start asking questions, talking, and paying attention to him so closely he's going to feel like he's under a microscope. Hopefully, that will stop him from doing stupid shit again."

"Hopefully," Tyler agrees.

"You've got my number if something happens. In the meantime, know we are keeping an eye on him. If he so much as sneezes in your direction, we'll deal with it." He pats Tyler's shoulder. "Sucks why I'm here, but it was nice seeing you two. And if anything else happens with the case, I'll let you know."

"Thanks." I give him a smile. I'm half-tempted to ask him if he's single and if he likes cupcakes, but I don't.

"Have a good night." He lifts his chin before he walks off.

"Well, now what?" I turn until I'm chest to chest with Tyler, and then I tip my head back to look at him and rest my hands on his chest.

"Now what?" He wraps his hands around my jaw.

"There's no more unknown bad guy. Your mom has come around and accepted that you're happy here. We're engaged and are going to move in together, even though we kinda already do live together."

"Yeah."

"So now what do we do?"

"Live our happily ever after."

"I like that idea," I agree with a smile as he leans down and presses his mouth to mine.

Suggestion 17

ENJOY THE MAGIC

TYLER

With a fresh cup of coffee, I head outside through the sliding glass doors and lean against the rail of the deck, taking in the beauty of Tennessee. This last year has flown by in a flash and, thankfully, has been mostly drama-free. Charles moved away from town two months after being arrested. Rumor was that his father's law firm had taken a hit because of his actions. To save his business, his dad couldn't keep him at the firm, but he did help him get a job in another state. I haven't heard anything about him since then, and honestly, that's okay with me.

Even though neither Leah nor Scott pressed charges against him, the kid who set the fire and trashed Leah's house still pled guilty to all the charges and served six months in jail. After he was released, he and his grandmother stopped by Leah's salon and apologized. Just like Leah, I felt bad for the kid. He was placed in an uncomfortable situation, where he had a really difficult decision to make: he had to choose between taking care of his family and letting harm come to them. He chose wrong, but in the end him admitting what he'd done spoke volumes for his character. From what I've heard, he's in college and doing community service. He's also paying restitution to the insurance company that covered the items destroyed in the fire by working part-time at a mechanic shop in town.

Heather is officially divorced from Marvin but isn't sure she'll be moving away from Montana anytime soon. The court ruled in her favor and granted her full custody of her daughter, but things between her and her ex have gotten better since her visit to see me, and she doesn't want Kennedy to grow up only seeing her father occasionally. According to my mom, Marvin's pulling out all the stops to win Heather back. Shockingly, my mom has been rooting for him to succeed. Maybe she feels guilty for the added stress she put on their marriage, or maybe she really thinks they have a shot at making things work. I just want my sister to be happy and can't wait to see her when she flies in tonight.

I take a sip of coffee as I look around the backyard of the cabin I rented for the week and inhale sharply when I glimpse Leah below. The first time I saw her sprawled out on the floor of my guest bedroom, she took my breath away, and every time I've seen her since then, she's had that same effect on me. Even today, dressed casually in tight jeans and high-heeled boots, she's the most stunning woman I've ever seen. She's waving her hands around as she talks to our moms. Tomorrow we're getting married, and the backyard of the cabin has been transformed by our mothers, who have steamrollered Leah and planned our wedding. Leah didn't want anything big, and while our moms acted like they agreed with her vision, I can now see from how the space is decorated that they didn't.

There's a podium set up underneath a large archway covered with fresh green pine, lights, and hundreds of gold, silver, and rose Christmas ball ornaments.

The chairs lining the aisle are decorated with the same green pine as well as white and gold ribbons and bows draped between each row. There are six—I know because I counted—Christmas trees decorated with the same color balls and lights as the arches lining the outside and the ends of the aisle, where a white mat will be rolled out for Leah to walk down to me after the sun sets. Off to the side there's a white tent set up with chairs, tables, and heaters to keep the outside space warm in winter. Even I have to admit the backyard looks amazing, but apparently my soon-to-be wife does not agree, judging by her flailing hands and the look on her beautiful face.

When both our mothers plant their hands on their hips, I know it's not gonna end well for my girl. I whistle, and the three women turn to look up at me. I only have eyes for one of them, and I crook my finger at her. I know she's sighing, even though I can't hear it, and her head shakes before she drops her eyes and leaves our moms outside.

I go inside as Leah stomps up the stairs, her high-heeled boots clipping hard against the wood, making her muttered words hard to distinguish.

"Really, Tyler, you call me up here when I'm attempting to talk sense into our mothers?" She angrily takes off her vest and tosses it to the couch. "Have you seen the backyard? There are Christmas trees outside! A lot of them!" She crosses her arms over her chest and glares at me.

"I like it." I shrug.

"You . . . you like it," she sputters in disbelief.

"You don't?" I question, moving closer to her.

"I thought we agreed on something small. There's at least two hundred chairs out there on the lawn." She waves to the window behind me.

"Baby." I wrap my arms around her, and she burrows into my chest.

"I thought . . . I thought our wedding would be small. Just family." She sounds exasperated.

"You should've known with our moms, it wouldn't be small."

"Why did I let them in on the planning?" She looks up at me.

"Because you didn't want to plan it. How many times did you skip out on meeting with them over the last year?"

She frowns at the reminder. "I've been busy."

She hasn't really been busy, unless you consider spending time with me and our families busy. She's had time to plan and make some arrangements, but if it were up to her, we would have gone to the courthouse and gotten married in front of the justice of the peace. "Baby."

"Don't 'baby' me, Tyler Duncan, you . . ." She points at me. "Even you have to admit that this is all way too much."

"I'm sorry, baby, but I don't agree."

Her head jerks back. "What?"

"I like the idea of our friends and our families watching us get married, watching you agree to be mine for the rest of our lives."

"So you like it because you're a caveman, over-the-top alpha male," she mutters, studying my face.

"Yep." I laugh, not even trying to deny it.

"Great," she sighs, dropping her forehead to my chest. "I'm screwed."

"We can give our mothers one day," I say, running my fingers through her hair and down her back.

"One day." Her head flies up so quickly it almost clips me in the jaw. "Are you insane? Next thing, they'll be dressing in all black, acting like ninjas, and confiscating my birth control so they can have another grandbaby to dote on." The image is too comical, so I throw my head back and start to laugh. "I'm not being funny," she cries, and I laugh louder. "Tyler!" Both her hands hit my chest, and I sober instantly and look into her beautiful eyes. Eyes I know I will love looking at today, tomorrow, and fifty years from now.

"I want a boy before a girl," I say. "That way, he can look out for his sister." Her expression gentles, and her body melts into mine. "I've told you before—I'd be happy if we had babies, and that hasn't changed. Really, I'm thinking the sooner the better."

"The sooner the better," she parrots, looking a little stunned, like we haven't had this exact conversation before.

"I'm not getting any younger, and neither are you. I figure we should start having babies soon."

"Babies," she whispers dreamily.

I smile while touching my mouth to her stunned lips. "You want kids, baby."

"I know, but only with you." Her assurance makes my chest warm.

"I want babies. Boys who are protective like me, and girls who look just like you."

Her eyes water, and it takes a moment for her to pull herself together. "You know," she says, smiling up at me, "it really sucks that you're better at changing the subject than I am."

"It wasn't really me who changed the subject," I point out.

She lets out a big breath before adding, "You're right, so we should go back to our previous conversation."

"Or we could move on," I say with a sigh.

"Just one more thing."

"All right, one more thing." I give her a squeeze.

"If our moms release doves tomorrow or have reindeer wandering around during the wedding, I reserve the right to say I told you so."

"Not sure there's any reindeer in Tennessee, baby."

"Oh, like that would stop those two. If they want reindeer at the wedding, I'm sure they'll have them flown in from wherever reindeer live."

I laugh and pull her tightly against me, then kiss the side of her neck. "How about this." I pull away to look at her. "If there are doves or reindeer tomorrow, I'll call everything off and take you to the courthouse in town."

"Deal," she agrees instantly, smiling.

I grin. "Now, with everyone occupied, how about you and I go upstairs?" I trail my hands down to her ass and press her hips against mine. "The reservation said that there's a sauna in the master bathroom. I figure we can disappear for a couple hours, and no one will notice."

Her voice is raspy when she whispers, "Lead the way."

I pick her up and carry her upstairs to the master bedroom and lock the door. I then proceed to take her mind off everything happening outside for a lot longer than two hours.

The next evening, with Scott at my side, I wait, like everyone else, for Leah to walk out the back door of the cabin. The sun has set, but the Christmas lights are glittering, so the space is filled with light—light that seems almost magical, like something from a fairy tale.

"It's time," our family pastor says, wrapping his hand around my shoulder, and I nod at him.

"Are you ready?" Scott asks, and I meet his gaze.

"Been ready." He smiles at me, then moves into place. I do the same, while the music starts up.

The back door of the cabin opens, and Chrissie steps outside, holding a bouquet of flowers close to her simple light-pink dress; then Leah's dad follows in a tux similar to mine. Leah appears in the open doorway, and my throat closes up at the sight of her in a formfitting white wedding dress. The top half is covered in lace from her chest down to her waist, and a fur shawl is tied around her shoulders with a silk ribbon at her throat. Her face is hidden by a veil, and her hair is down around her shoulders.

"Lucky bastard," Scott mutters under his breath, and I smile. He's right. I'm one lucky bastard. I found something rare. I found the love of a good woman—a woman I look forward to spending the rest of my life with. Best of all, I wasn't even looking . . . she literally fell through my window.

When Leah and her father reach the podium, I move forward to shake his hand.

"I don't need to tell you to take care of her. I already know you will." Her dad claps me on the shoulder before he kisses Leah's cheek over her veil and whispers something to her. When he pulls back and looks at me, his eyes are teary.

"I got her from here." He lifts his chin, and I take Leah's hand. I help her up the two steps to the podium, and once we're in place, I look down at her, hating the veil between us. Pastor Rodsend starts to speak, and it seems to take forever to get to the part I'm looking forward to most. When he says the words I've been waiting to hear, I say, "I do," and listen to Leah repeat the same words before I lift the soft fabric away from her face. I look into her eyes, feeling my throat begin to close once more.

"Hey," she whispers, looking at me nervously, like we're strangers, and I fight back the sudden urge to laugh.

When I have myself under control, I whisper back, "You look amazing. You're always beautiful and always have a way of stopping my breath and giving it back to me, but right now . . ." I shake my head. "Jesus, baby, you stop my heart from beating."

"Tyler." Her body melts into mine.

"You're everything, everything to me, Leah." I capture her face in my hands.

"You're everything to me too." She licks her lips and drops her eyes to my mouth. "Now, would you fricking kiss me already?"

"Can't a guy enjoy the view for a moment?" I tease.

She shakes her head no, and then, surprising me, she leans up on her tiptoes and grabs my face. She pulls my lips to hers, and even though I'm caught off guard, the kiss is not a quick touch of our lips. It's wild and deep and everything a kiss should be. We're both breathing heavily when she pulls her mouth from mine, and I hear her faint whispered "Oh my goodness" over the shouts from our family and friends as she tucks her face into my neck. I laugh, holding her close, then swing her up into my arms and listen to her squeak as she wraps her arms around my neck. The shouting gets louder as I carry her down the aisle, but neither of us hears anything after I cart my new wife inside to make out with her.

Epilogue

THREE YEARS LATER

TYLER

I pull into the garage and grab dinner from the passenger seat before I get out of my truck. As soon as I open the door, I hear Leah shouting, "Stop running away from me and put on your clothes." I pause at the end of the hall, watching my almost-three-year-old daughter, Cori (short for Corina), run past me completely naked, with her mom chasing after her, holding a pair of little girl's underwear in one hand and a shirt in the other. By the time I hit the living room, Leah has trapped our girl and has forced her into her underwear and is attempting to put a T-shirt on her. I'm not surprised by this situation; Cori would run around naked all the time if we allowed it.

"Cori, why are you giving your mama a hard time?" I look at my girl, who's hanging half–upside down off the ottoman next to the couch, trying to get out of putting on her shirt.

"Daddy," she shrieks when her beautiful eyes lock with mine. Then she shoots up to stand before jumping into my arms.

I balance her and the bag of food in my grasp, then look at my wife. When she rests her hands on her swollen stomach and lets out a sigh, I smile at her, and she smiles back.

"How are all my girls today?"

"Good," Cori says, looking up at me and smiling before resting her head against my shoulder and wrapping her arms around my neck.

I look from her to Leah, and she shakes her head. She touches Cori's hair and rests her hand on her stomach. "Between this wild one and her dancing on my bladder day and night, I'm not sure I have it in me to try again for the boy you want." She's full of shit. Yes, our girl's wild, and yes, the daughter who'll be joining us in three short months is causing her to run to the restroom every few minutes, but I know, just like me, she's happy in our chaos and happy with the life we've built.

"I want a brother," Cori informs us while looking at Leah's stomach like she has the power to change the sex of her sister.

"Maybe someday, honey." Leah laughs and kisses the side of her head when she pouts.

I lean over and kiss the top of Leah's head, then inform Cori, "You need to finish getting dressed so you can eat." I take her shirt from Leah before going to the kitchen. Bruce, like always, is sprawled out on the kitchen floor and hardly lifts his head to acknowledge our presence. He's used to the chaos, whereas Mouse avoids it at all costs by staying hidden until Cori is asleep for the night. I set the bag with dinner on the counter, then put Cori down and help her into her shirt. When she's covered, I carry her to her high chair and lock her in so she can't escape and climb onto the kitchen table to sing or dance, which she does often when we're not overly careful. I hand her my cell phone so she can watch her favorite videos on YouTube. Once she's settled, I go to Leah, who's making our plates, and take advantage of the few minutes of quiet to feel her up and steal a few kisses. I've missed her today. Hell, I miss her when I haven't seen her for just a few hours. My obsession with her hasn't changed over the last few years, even after us becoming parents.

"Your mom called me this morning," Leah says after we've sat down and she's dug into her Chinese food. I study her expression, hoping my mom didn't ruin the surprise. "She says she and your dad will be here tomorrow evening. She asked if I wanted her to pick up the Tennessee wine my mom loved from that shop in town."

"Shit."

"Daddy said a bad word," Cori informs Leah, briefly looking up from her show to tattle on me.

Leah smiles at our girl and pats the top of her hand before she looks at me once more. "Did you forget to tell me something?"

I play it off and explain. "Mom and Dad are missing their grand-baby. I forgot to tell you that they called a few days ago and are coming this weekend to spend time with her."

"Then we're not going away to Jamaica, and I don't need to buy a new swimsuit?" I close my eyes in frustration because I should never have told my mom my plan to get Leah alone for a few days before she can't travel. "She didn't tell me," she says, and I open my eyes to look at her. "I saw the travel plans in an email over a month ago."

"Sneak." I give her a little glare, and she smiles innocently.

"Honestly, it's just good to know you're not sneaking off with a mistress." Her tone is joking, but there's an undercurrent of truth in it.

I frown and then shake my head. "You're not serious."

"I'm fat," she states, and I feel a rumble of aggravation deep in my chest. "I don't look—"

"You're still the most beautiful woman I've ever seen in my life. You're not . . ." I look down at Cori and cut myself off before I curse. "You're not fat. You're creating a life inside you—a life I had a hand in making."

Her face softens, and I get up from my chair and go to her. I pull her up to stand in front of me. I hold her face in my hands, then drop my face closer to hers. "Never doubt that you're my world. That our family is what makes my world turn. Without you and my girls, I'd be lost." I move one hand to rest on her stomach. "I love my life and our family, and I would never—not ever—do anything to jeopardize that."

"Okay," she whispers, holding my gaze.

"Our trip was supposed to be a surprise."

"I have work and—"

I cut her off. "Your mom and grandma already got everything you'll need and have spoken with your clients. It's all set."

"Of course they have," she mumbles.

I ignore her comment. "I want us to have time to reconnect before Lacy gets here." I rub her stomach. "You've been working hard, and between me, Cori, the shop, your family, and mine, you don't take time for yourself."

Her brow furrows. "I love our family. It's not a hardship to take care of you guys."

"I know that, but I want to take care of you. I *need* to take care of you." I tighten my hand around her jaw. "Let me."

"You do take care of me. You always take care of me and our family."

"Then let me continue to do that. Pretend like you never saw that email and act surprised when we go to the airport."

"I'm not sure I can pretend. It's a nice resort, though. The room looks awesome, and I've been thinking about the beach for a month now." She grins and I laugh.

I drop my mouth to her ear. "The room and the beach aren't exactly what I've been thinking about when it comes to having you alone for a few days."

"Right, I forgot to mention sleeping," she jokes, sounding breathless.

"I can promise you'll sleep, but only after I have my way with you." I kiss the shell of her ear, and she groans in response. I pull back to look into her eyes. "I love you, baby."

"I love you too." She leans up on her tiptoes, pressing her mouth to mine. I hold her against me, taking everything she's willing to give, and only when Cori interrupts us with a loud "Stop kissing" do I pull away. I look from my wife's beautiful face to my baby's and know I have it all—everything I ever wished for.

LEAH

With the sun warm on my skin and the scent of salt water in the air, I turn my head to the side and look at my husband. Tyler in his everyday jeans and tee is hot. Tyler in nothing but swim shorts, displaying his toned, tan torso, is a sight to behold. He was right—we needed this, time alone, time just for us. I love our life, I love being a mom, but I also enjoy the rare times I get to spend alone with my husband. Since we got married and had Corina, there hasn't been a lot of time for us to just be . . . well, us. Until we got to Jamaica and checked into our room—not having to think about bath time, bedtime, or the million other things that come along with parenthood—I didn't realize how much I missed just being me. A woman married to a hot guy.

"The only thing that would make this trip better are nonvirgin piña coladas," I say with a sigh, rolling to my side since I can't comfortably lie on my stomach.

At my comment, Tyler lifts his head and pushes his sunglasses up into his hair to look at me. "Baby . . . you, sunshine, and alcohol don't mix, or do I need to remind you of our honeymoon?"

"Our honeymoon," I parrot. "A week of sun, sand, and hot sex."

"The first day, you were hungover."

"Yes." But just that first day. After that I learned not to drink so much while spending time under the hot sun. "Hot, dirty, drunk sex was phenomenal," I remind him.

His eyes light in a different way. "You got me there." His grin and his large hand coming to rest on my hip make my stomach flutter. "I'm pretty sure you don't need a drink to get dirty for me."

"No, I don't think I do," I whisper as his palm snakes up my side to rest just under my breast.

"Let's see if that's true," he rumbles before he kisses me. Then he pulls me from my lounger and takes me inside to our room, where he proves I don't need a drink to get dirty for him.

Four days later, feeling relaxed and revitalized, we pull into our garage. As soon as I open my car door, he's there to take my hand in his, and I smile while he places a soft kiss on my lips. When we get inside, our beautiful girl runs to us down the hall, shrieking, "Mommy and Daddy are home!" while she throws herself into us. Tyler picks her up, and we hold her between us, showering kisses on her chubby cheeks and listening to her say how much she's missed us. I look at my husband over our daughter's head and know I found my happily ever after and that I caught something beautiful when I caught the guy next door.

Acknowledgments

First, I have to give thanks to God, because without him none of this would be possible. Second, I want to thank my husband. I love you now and always—thank you for believing in me, even when I don't always believe in myself. To my beautiful son, you bring such joy into my life, and I'm so honored to be your mom.

To everyone who reads or writes blogs and loves books, thank you for taking the time to read and share mine. There will never be enough ink in the world to acknowledge you all, but I will forever be grateful to each and every one of you.

Like thousands of authors before me, I started this writing journey after I fell in love with reading. I wanted to give people a place to escape where the stories were funny, sweet, and hot and left them feeling good. I've loved sharing my stories with you all, loved that I've helped people escape the real world, even for a moment.

I started writing for me and will continue writing for you.

XOXO,

Aurora

About the Author

Aurora Rose Reynolds is a *New York Times* and *USA Today* bestselling author whose wildly popular series include Fluke My Life, Until, Until Him, Until Her, and Underground Kings. Her writing career started as an attempt to get the outrageous alpha men in her head to leave her alone and has blossomed into an opportunity to share her stories with readers all over the world.

To stay up to date on what's happening, join the Alpha Mailing List: https://bit.ly/2GXYsVS. To order signed books, go to https://AuroraRoseReynolds.com. You can reach Reynolds via email at Auroraroser@gmail.com and follow her on Instagram (@Auroraroser), Facebook (AuthorAuroraRoseReynolds), and Twitter (@Auroraroser).